Temporary Lives

Temporary Lives

and other stories

Ramola D

University of Massachusetts Press
AMHERST AND BOSTON

LC 2009040306
ISBN 978-1-55849-742-9 (cloth)

Designed by Kristina Kachele
Set in Arnhem Blond with Arnhem Fine display
Printed and bound by Thomson-Shore, Inc.

Library of Congress Cataloging-in-Publication Data
D, Ramola, 1964– .
Temporary lives and other stories / by Ramola D.
p. cm. — (Grace Paley prize in short fiction)
ISBN 978-1-55849-742-9 (cloth : alk. paper)
I. Title.
PS3554.H27T46 2010
813'.54—dc22
2009040306

British Library Cataloguing in Publication data are available.

for my darling Sophie,
forever

I wish that every human life
might be pure transparent freedom.
SIMONE DE BEAUVOIR

Acknowledgments

໓ I would like to thank the editors who have supported and encouraged my work through publication, especially, from way back, Matt Friedson and Jenine Gordon, and, more recently, Felicia Sullivan, Hilda Raz, and Leslie Daniels. Thanks also to writers A. M. Holmes, Stephen King, and editors Susan Burmeister-Brown and Linda Swanson-Davies of *Glimmer Train,* who have otherwise recognized my work, in contests and listings; to Matthew Cheney and Jeff and Ann VanderMeer, who included a story in *Best American Fantasy 2007;* to writer Richard Bausch, my first fiction teacher in the United States; and to writer Sandra Cisneros for her invitation to the intense and inspiring experience of Macondo. I would like to thank also the National Endowment for the Arts for their 2005 award in poetry, which has both created time and encouraged me immensely to continue writing, both poetry and fiction. Very special thanks to AWP, to the University of Massachusetts Press, and to writers Jewell Parker-Rhodes as also Rigoberto Gonzalez, who, incredibly, selected this manuscript for the 2008 Grace Paley Prize and so have made this publication possible. My deepest gratitude to all at UMass Press, especially Bruce Wilcox, Carol Betsch, Sally Nichols, Kristina Kachele, and Carla Potts, for their thoughtfulness and creativity, not to mention all the hard work expended in the production of this book. It's been extraordinary working together on its creation, including painting a possible cover in the middle of a hectic summer. And, because I do subscribe to the notion of trace and residue and lingerings, I would like to thank some of the many writers who have gone before, who inspire and teach me to write, especially Janet Frame, Marguerite Duras, Kate Braverman, Carole Maso, Sandra Cisneros, Toni Morrison, Gabriel Garcia Marquez, and Franz Kafka. I am grateful to my family, especially Paul, for enduring and supporting my writing in all those years of writing into the dark.

Some of these stories originally appeared in magazines.
"In Another World" in *Hyper Age*
"The Man on the Veranda" in *Small Spiral Notebook*
(Received an Honorable Mention in the 2003 *Zoetrope*
Short Fiction Contest)
"Same Blue Sky" in *So to Speak*
"Temporary Lives" in *Prairie Schooner*
"The Next Corpse Collector" in *Green Mountains Review*
(Reprinted in *Best American Fantasy 2007*; listed in 100 Other
Distinguished Stories in *Best American Short Stories, 2007*)
"Esther" was a finalist in the January 2008 *Glimmer Train* Family
Matters Contest.

Contents

Temporary Lives

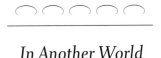

In Another World

و۔ My sister says she is never lonely. She means inside, where the heart is, where I feel in myself a dim roar and pulse, erratic cessation and return that pours chaos into me. She says she carries her true life inside her. That violet worlds erupt at her fingertips. That they reach into being like threads of light from distant stars, delicate in their entrance but powerful. She tells me roses hued cadmium red spill into her arms. Their scent rising like a cloud of forgotten things swarming about her body. She is alone, a woman in a magic landscape.

I look at our two selves in the mirror, our dark hair, our bright eyes. Her image is swollen with the child inside and her eyes are still upon herself, as if she were seeing a body quiet and dead before her. Her eyes are brown pools of stagnant water.

Yes, and on the surface I see birds, dead birds, their wings arrested in flight, beaks turned sadly downward, their pained feathers rustling. They are lonely in death, and shrunken and weighted, as if the distance kept between their living selves had grown, consumed them. On the water there are leaves, and parts of leaves. Veins, skeletal. Umber and olive, drifting. On the water is the face of a terrible calm. It lies as if asleep, long hands afloat behind its fallen head, eyes closed eternally upon themselves. There is no wind. But a breath, a whisper of breath slipping outward from dead mouths.

Far below, where lucence slips into green desolation, a spiral of water lifts. It pours into and out of itself, there, deep beneath the skin.

My sister looks at her reflection in the cracked mirror in the empty daytime house with the crows cawing in the courtyard and the aluminum clatter of vessels in the neighboring compound and her reflection turns her purely into herself. I know there is movement there, orange silk twisting by itself in wind, even dancing. But it is hidden.

My sister tells me she is never lonely and I believe her. Her eyes are pinned on the world, its myriad failings. But they are turned inward.

When the nubbing lisp of pain comes through my chest, whorls and rosettes of pain, stones and round hills of pain, and stands there calmly as bread, I put my hand to the tender aureoles, the sharp cones of the nipples, I try to hold the pain in my hands, still the growing with my hands, and she looks at me.

They won't go away, she says. They won't return to where they came from.

I never wanted breasts, I say. I didn't ask for them.

She begins to smile then. She turns her empty hands palm upward to the blue impervious sky, its wrappings of light glancing off her covered shoulders, her plain and shining skin, she smiles. In the courtyard where the clothes are strung on thin jute rope between the lime and the guava trees, and the bunches of shade and blouses swing loosely in the wind, and the quiet sleeps between us like an ocean, she says to me, you are a child, you know nothing yet, isn't it plain, *you cannot want.*

I wake from a dream in which the small pile of oranges kept beneath the plastic lid of the onion basket in the kitchen grows till they fill the room, great rippling skins of oranges flowing till they touch the ceiling and swallow the light bulb and its yellow light, round fervor of oranges squandered, ruptured, squeezing through the narrow doorway and the old windows till the juice in them begins to *drip, drip, drip,* and the sting and citrus scent of them spills into my nostrils, I wake with a start. My sister is sitting beside me on the narrow cot, her pregnant stomach under her cotton saree huge in the thin light from the street lamp outside, her ringed hands peeling and peeling. She is peeling an orange.

Then she sees me awake like that, eyes flared open, face still buried in the dream, and the scent of it rising and growing around us like a sin, she says, you're not to tell anyone, do you hear?

I shake my head. In that light, watery and gray, the shadows flittering around us like droves of dying moths and the small hanging crib with the baby in it swinging a little as if it were possible always to live like that, sleeping, watched over, cotton mounds of pain growing on my chest, I feel as if I am a small way inside her world. She has come home to have her third child. She is eight and a half months pregnant. I know she wakes sometimes like that, with a terrible craving for food. But the oranges are not hers. They are kept for my brother.

In the house across the street from us there are four boys and two girls. I know the girls are married and have children and live in their husbands' houses. Ali, the oldest, ran away from home at sixteen and never returned. I hear the stories his father tells, how he believes his son has caught a train to the south and is limping from hospital to hospital, looking for help and medicine.

For Ali, like all the others in the family, has a form of schizophrenia. They have inherited it from their mother, and from their father's father. I have seen their mother sit on the tiny stone veranda of their house, leaning against the concrete pillar by the steps, eyes open and staring. She never speaks to us. I sit across the street from her by the window that looks onto the street and see how the world enters and flails and disappears in her eyes. Sometimes she puts a hand to her head to scratch at the uncombed hair and forgets to bring it down. Sometimes she sings. The song comes to me paperthin and bleak, curling round the edges in the heat, voice darkening and rasping, her words pulled like beads from the swollen strings of air afloat about her.

Ahmed is the youngest. He tells me of the cheetahs and saints and devils lurking everywhere—in the walls, behind his bed, in the air over my shoulder when I speak to him. They are like swarms of red ants or locusts buzzing and spinning about his ears, they besiege him. Often he cowers against the wall, elbows raised above his head, covering his ears. When my brother and I go into their house to play, we see him crouched in terror against the wall, shuddering and muttering, holding back the avalanche of evil beings that linger and shake and rave about him. Then we turn and look for these phantoms, our own skin alive with fear, and there is nothing. Sunlight, a fold of shadow. Then nothing. *But Ahmed can see them.*

Farid is a manic-depressive. I have learned this means he often surges into excessive rage that no one can control. It is best then to be nowhere near him. My mother calls for us to stop playing in the dusty street and come into the house. She bolts the door and shuts the lower half of the window. We climb on the windowsill and kneel and look through the upper half, hiding our faces behind the thin saree-curtain when he looks our way. That is how we see him tearing down the front door one day, grasping its wooden halves in such passion that the wood splinters and cracks and the hinges break, and the slow creaking whine the hinges make lingers in the weeping air a long time after.

I know there are days when he sits as still as his mother. When his eyes are closed windows in a dead house. Gaze swimming as if in narrow circles inside a stoppered bottle with spent air. He is nearer then to us, a giant calmed. We speak to him. Shred daisies on his hands, bury petals in his hair. He talks to himself, avoiding our gaze. He shifts under our attentions. But a small warm current of affection flows between us.

I think of his father, how he must sit, up in the guard tower at the Kasimpur railway station, waving the trains on, slowly, meticulously, the green cotton flag, the crimson flare, how the gods and lucifers and satans of his children's visions must pass before him like crowned and haloed figures from a dream, how he lets them pass on the sizzling tracks they share with the diesels and the coal engines, how the *chug chug* of their departing selves makes patterns of black and red on the smog-filled horizon. Farid's father is not like ours. He is gentle, he cares for the family. It is he who takes the children to the hospital, makes certain they take their pills. Nights when he comes home, it is he who puts the pots of rice and parripu on the fire and cooks the evening meal. I like their father.

But Hamid, it is Hamid I love.

When we were small, Hamid took us, my little brother and myself, to the marketplace.

He bought us little cubes and pyramids of jaggery, dark sugar that melted in our mouths. He took us to the spice stall where we stood looking at the mounds of brilliant yellow turmeric, the red chili powder, the brown coriander, the black pepper, wanting to plunge our hands into the pristine cones of color, inhale the forest scent of cloves, cardamom, anise.

He held our hands as we stepped across slivers of skin or bone at the meat market and stared, holding our breath, at the skinned sides of goats, the way the veins, dark blue, lay thinly under the surface, as blue as if alive. His uncle worked at the meat stall. He would lean down and talk to us, buy us sticky swirls of jilebi that dripped molten sugar on our clothes.

Hamid was ten years older than my sister, who is six years older than me. My mother would not let my sister go with us on our trips to the marketplace. My sister was already grown, she said. She could not play with boys anymore. Besides, Hamid was a grown man, what was he doing, playing like a child? It was not proper.

It is true Hamid played with us as if he were a child. He taught us to make kites, to powder bottle-glass and mix it with glue before we dipped the twine in it and strung it out to dry so our kite-strings would be the deadliest on the street. When we hoisted our brilliant squares and diamonds of grape and gas-blue into the sky, the strings hissed as they rose, they tangled high with the neighborhood kites and cut them, string against string, easy as knife-edge, till they broke, paper and bamboo holds plummeting.

Those were his good days. When Hamid was in his depression no one could find him.

My sister says that he went to the movies with his friends. He stole money from his mother to go to the movies. He sank himself in the enchanted worlds they opened up to him. For the women in the movies were beautiful. The places they showed were beautiful. The men did wild, incredible stunts with precipices, fast cars, and burning buildings. Something about the glamour of the movies, the fantasy of those other lives, the actors living charmed lives in their mansions enslaved him.

Now I hear his father say he takes drugs, strange powders, ganja and hashish, that steal into his mind and create visions for him. He sits on the veranda with a dumb smile on his face, he smiles into the sleeping street. Sometimes he sleeps. He lies in the inner chamber of the house, where the boys sleep, all through the day he lies on a mat on the cool floor, he sleeps.

My little brother, who is the youngest of my brothers, who are all older than I, has become a person I cannot recognize. His face is sharp with dark bristles, shadows etched on his chin. His eyes are brooding and melancholy. When he speaks, his voice pitches forward in a daze and cannot retrieve itself.

But he has learned the language of men. When he speaks, something inside me shakes a little, as if in disbelief, in grieving. I try to laugh at him, but he frowns, his face pinches up into crooked lines. He reminds me he is older than I am. He tells me I cannot laugh like this, it is not becoming. He tells me he is there to tell me these things, to protect me. He says *you must believe me.*

And so there are days I steal into the house when Hamid sleeps and Ahmed is away at the Corporation school and Farid at work at the steel factory and their mother lies in a stupor in the midday heat, I come into the room where the dark pools and huddles, I sit beside

Hamid where he sleeps and I watch his heaving body, his chest rise and fall, his breath escape in a slow sigh through his shiny nostrils. The heat from his body rises and stands between us. I look at the smooth muscles on his arm and chest, his long legs, his sleeping mouth, and my heart contracts. I feel in my soul the deep and sweeping emptiness that Hamid feels. I think he is lost in sleep like this, lost in green worlds too submerged, too hidden for me to enter because he is lonely.

Each morning I wake, I boil the water for the tea, I bring it in tumblers to my father, my brothers, their wives, their children. I bring water from the street pump in the brass pot kept there all morning in the long queue in the street, I sit with my sisters-in-law in the kitchen, we make breakfast. I clean the rice, break the coconut, crush the spices, and boil the lentils for our midday meal. I used to go to school, like my sister did, but I am needed in the house now.

No one speaks to me because I am too old to be a child, too young to be a woman.

When I sit in that dark room with fingers of light reaching from the bars and lying in smudges of gold on our limbs, I feel as if I am a nurse in a hospital, an angel in human guise, guarding the sleep of the near-dead or the dying. I think his body is a stone covered with water, a round stone, sunk to the bottom of a dark pool. I think each time his soul hovers, high above his body, dreaming of leaving. I think how he is like my sister, his mind slipping deep, deep, into worlds of his own, stars exploding at his touch, deserts bursting into flower and water. More and more each day he lies like that, sleeping and dreaming and sweating, and I watch him.

One day I touch him. Something shakes in that space between his skin and mine, something I cannot put a name to. Sweat comes off on my hands. With dirt.

My sister does not know this.

But sometimes Hamid wakes when I am there beside him. When Hamid wakes he turns, he smiles at me. Then I lean against him.

I go to their house through the door that opens on the alley behind. Ahmed and his mother are used to me. They let me come and go as I please. Sometimes I bring them food from our house, and they like that.

My sister sits with her head turned toward the wall in the courtyard when I return, and the small leaf-shadows on the wall turn and tremble in the wind. I sit beside her. I watch her when she speaks.

In another world, my sister is radiant. Her body lifts her clear above shadow and she laughs, she laughs constantly. *Want,* she whispers, *you must want. Didn't you know this,* she says, *isn't it plain, can't you see, without wanting, there is no life.*

My sister was fifteen when she was married. Now she carries a child, her third child in four years. The skin of her face and breasts sags a little. I have seen her stand in the bathroom where the light comes in a slit from the window high above, her feet slipping on the floor, hands reaching to the walls to steady her body. When the water pours from the mug over her face, her thin body with the swell of her stomach gleaming, I think she is like a silver coin in a dark room, light a wisp of straw on her face, I think she is beautiful.

She rocks the two baby girls one after the other in the crib that hangs from the ceiling. She speaks to no one.

When I ask her why, why another, she looks at me for a long time without saying anything. Her mouth is bitter in its tightness.

For a moment I linger. I feel I am walking on an edge, a fine sharp edge, below which there are rocks, and no trees, and a chasm. Then I know this is a dangerous place.

I remember my own darkness, two months ago, that spilling of the child's dream, that plunge into vertigo, first awareness of death. And I draw back, remembering.

It was the first time the sac cracked and tore in me and the blood spilled, long muslin threads of red, flakes and layers, wet knots and pellets of red, a cupful of blood gathering in streaks on the voile pads she made for me from her old sarees. I thought I was going to die.

This is how it began, I thought, the dark growth, the spilling.

Cancer, I had heard the word *cancer.* I knew what it meant. It meant death, bleeding. Open mouth in a dark room, the stain of drying blood on old cloth, the body turned viciously upon itself.

My sister saw the stain on my skirt and led me to the bathroom. No one had told me what this meant, I said.

It means your body is no longer yours, she said. It means that babies can form, round and firm, like fruit inside you.

I thought only married women could have children, I said.

She looked darkly at me, pinpricks of flame in her eyes. You are so young, she said, so young! You don't have to be married to have a child.

That is when I began to worry. Seeds can fall inside you and take root and grow, she said. Before you know it, your stomach will be swollen, and you cannot hide it.

The shame, I thought. *The shame.*

Seeds from where?

From men, she said. Seeds from men.

I thought of that, men planting the seeds, turning the earth over. The earth?

In you, she said. They can plant the seeds in you. That is why you should not be with men, ever. Not until you are married. Because it can happen anytime.

In me?

See how that spills, she said. See where it spills from? In there!

I looked down at myself, the deep cleft, the darkness.

There's a place inside you where the baby will form, she said, sleep and grow. Then it will come down through there and be born.

Through here? This trickling of space, this narrowness? I had thought they cut stomachs open and fished babies out, alive and gasping for air.

Through there, she said. Now clean yourself and put this on.

I felt the walls of my womb contract then, felt the heavy rush and surge of blood as it was expelled. I saw now why my mother had kept such a sharp eye on my sister while we were growing up.

Yes, I thought of Hamid, his body damp and burning against mine. And I was afraid.

My sister has been to the hospital three times this week. She is due next Monday. Complications, the doctor says. The head hasn't turned, my sister says. But she doesn't sound worried.

So I sit with her in the twilight in the courtyard and we count the parrots that come, screeching, to light on the guava trees. She combs my hair like she used to, and I play idly with the glass bangles on my hands.

Some days, with everyone asleep in the afternoons, I go out alone and sit under the lime tree in the courtyard.

Under the lime tree on cracked earth, drizzle of lime flowers, pressed yellow and white. Small crumple of flower in my hands. I touch the petals, crinkling of paper and edge, the nubbed centers.

I feel the stream of red heat rise inside me, a small coiled serpent of heat, tearing and flaring, light shredding at edges. It eats like termite hunger through my limbs, chewing and spitting.

I have felt nothing like this before. It is dizzying and sharp, a thin cold blade sucked in through the lungs and turning and turning. My body pulls in upon itself and lets go, pulls in, lets go, like the wild spasms of the ocean, waves incessant. I feel the ribs under my new breasts. They pulse in my hands like stars. Is this pain, is it desire?

It is midday. The heat is March heat, sun-climb into affliction.

The day it happens, no one is prepared. But what could be a preparing? My sister's baby is born, a breached birth, a son. My sister's body, bright, famished body, sick with knowledge, yields, yields and stills. The doctors tell us *she was too weak, she was not prepared, she was undernourished, she had no strength, she lost too much blood.*

In the blue peeling rooms of the hospital with the corridors of scabbed bodies and eaten limbs my sister lies.

My mother weeps, my father beats upon his chest. My brother-in-law is stricken and heroic, his eyes full with emotion.

But a son was born. The tears are not pure. There is rejoicing.

When I close my eyes now I no longer dream. I am hungry for dream, its smooth and open spaces, its oiled skin sliding gently over mine, blue and green, inviting. I am thirsty for ocean-water from another world, dark skies, stars frothing in sparks on my skin. My eyes hurt when I wake—thin layers of skin, eyelids starved and dry—hurt like veins pulled from leaves and burning, pulled from world into negation, chapter of closings, litany of ends.

My sister is asleep, round berry asleep in the sun. Her mouth is closed upon innocence. Her eyes move gently in her dream like long strands of seaweed in water. I know she has slipped already into the water on the other side of the light, her long legs cast a shadow. She is swimming so far from me I fear I cannot reach her. Wait, I say, wait for me. And I run, but the water comes between us like a wall of glowing. I cannot swim, I reach with swollen hands, I flounder. The water pours into my face and mouth and eyes, it stills and stops my lungs. I kick and rise, cup and press, I walk backward from the water.

My sister is asleep in another world. Her voice is passing into wind, her hands are swirling and twisting. They are making the shapes of things I have never seen, speaking in words I cannot hear. The light is dark and light all at once, a flashing of greens and blues, a thatched and covered ocher. My hands are tight in Hamid's hands, his mouth is covering mine. I am lonely for her world. I am lonely for the dark she wore about her like a veil, the flare of radiance at her fingertips. In the dark of the inner room I am trying so hard to reach her, my hands pushing through the water like knives, my eyes stinging, my heart looking forever for the roses to spill, the desert to open, to swallow me whole.

The Next Corpse Collector

꒰ My brother Anwar brings the mangled body in with my father. The red checked shirt is wet with blood, black cotton pant torn at the knees where the bones have slid through. They lay the body on the wooden bench in the courtyard, beside the one drumstick tree that is still standing. The arms hang down and they lift them. The left foot slips, they pull it back, close. They have already closed the eyes. They do not glance at each other. They stand and look down on the body.

It is no secret in our house that Anwar is the favored one, the one my father loves, whom my father looked, early, in the eyes and said, You will be the one who will carry on my work in your life. He meant the work of collecting corpses, from the hospitals and police stations, the bodies of those who lived on the streets, who had no one to sign their papers, dress their bodies for burial, take them to their final resting-place. My father did this for them. He waited outside the hospitals for the summons to pick up the body. With the help of the orderlies or the peons, he loaded the body into the rickshaw, put up the black vinyl cover, and cycled up to the Krishna Raja crematorium by the Krishna temple in Mylapore if they were Hindus or to the Inshallah cemetery in Kilpauk if they were Muslims. He avoided the main roads, seeking out the tight alleys and side-roads, past houses and small shops. He wanted to spare the living, but usually the body was well enough covered that it could pass for a sack of tapioca roots from the vegetable market, or, if reclined, like a sick person going to the doctor.

Sometimes he brought the body home first. He would lay it out in our cramped courtyard, beside the two drumstick trees in the center, and wash and dress it. He put clothes on the body his mosque supplied as a service to the dead, clean white dhotis and long voile shirts on the men, cheap, colored Coimbatore cotton sarees on the women. My mother helped him then. And we did, too, Anwar and I, from very young, we were raised like this, among the living and the dead, it was not strange to us to wipe the whole, wet body down with a cloth, or to pull a comb through the matted hair of a corpse.

It is true the first time I saw one come through the wooden doorway and lie there in the sunlight on the cracked cement I was silenced. The round noon shadow of the drumstick trees by his foot was tight and dark on his skin. I know I was young, very young, how young I do not know. The shadows of things were large then. All bodies had weight. The house loomed around me like the inside of a giant shell. The walls were tall, ceilings high. This was long before the house began to shrink into the toy shape it now holds, the cramped restlessness. I had never seen before such absolute stillness in any creature. It was like a sleep that was so deep and folded under itself it could not be touched.

And yet, he was human. I was afraid, because of this—he was a person, like any of us. He might wake at any moment, sit, open his eyes. But he was dead, he was not supposed to, it would be grotesque. He could make his face into a buffalo-demon mask or make his eyes go wide or reach out and squeeze our throats. Being dead all the time, and the horror held me still. My father beckoned me close but I hung back. I waited till they had begun to wash him before I approached. I saw a tuft of black curly hair first, smooth dark sheen to the skin, a layer of moisture on the face where my father had wiped it. A smell rose, sharp and strange, like Dettol, or the tight iron smell of new blood, in a market. I came slowly close, held my breath. The eyes were lidded down, a wet sparkle of eye showing through the tight toothbrush lashes, mouth hanging slightly open. The bluish red tongue lolled to one side. It was a man, I saw, a young man.

So young, my mother murmured, as she brought a bucket of water to the body and sat beside him. His arms were thin, legs beneath the dhoti dark. I thought he might have been a rickshaw-wallah, the muscles on his calf were tight and bulged. His body was splayed—arms out, legs out, everything spread, as if in defiance of us, the living. Or maybe just in completion, a natural arrogance a person acquires in the deep repose of such sleep, an unselfconsciousness. How did he die, my mother asked, rubbing a wet cloth over his chest. He drank himself to death, my father said. The Rampet police found him lying on his face right outside the toddy shop, in the side by the dustbin, where the pigs live. It's the toddy I smell, then, my mother said, taking her pallu across her nose and chin and tucking it into her shoulder.

I did not come too close. I saw the dry, chapped soles, bruise of bluish-green on the big toe, long, in-curved nails with the dirt under them. His body remained ordinary, alive. I was still afraid he might get up or open his eyes. My heart beat in my chest so loud, like a trapped moth lost in our room at night, I thought it might wake him. So I kept my distance.

But after that day I was not so afraid of the bodies that came to our house looking for that last wash, a hair-combing, clean bowels, and a fresh set of clothes to wear into the next world.

I watched from the door instead, while Anwar helped, and my mother cleaned and carried away the waste in a closed pan, and my father went methodically over the tasks of pressing the lower abdomen to evict the waste, wiping, washing, clothing the person dead.

Fragments. I picked up fragments. Sometimes whole sentences. I would hear my father say to Anwar, see, this is how, and never leave the police station without this information. Always ask where the body was found, and by whom and how. Always note the time of death, this is important. Because the decay will start otherwise—you need to know when to be ready for it.

And the rigor mortis—you have to be able to move the limbs and push the muscles if you are going to clean the body.

My father never noticed me then, in those days. I hid behind a curtain or a door, trying to hear. It was like being in a school, but just outside the classroom. I ran my hands over the blue peeling wash covering the brick in the outside wall, sucked in the hot sun-smell of the courtyard, and kept still, so they would not know I was crouched there, listening. Anwar worked as if born to the act of service, pouring a bucket of water over the legs, hurrying around to the shoulder or the chest, wiping the face, smoothing the wet hair and fanning it with a dried palm-leaf fan. He was quiet and quick on his feet, which my father praised him for. Time is gold, he would say to him, in our profession, Time is of the essence. If Time is not on our side, we lose. If we spend our Time wisely, we win.

What do we win, he would then ask, like a schoolmaster. We win our fight against Death, Anwar would respond, mechanically. And I would watch them both half-lift, half-drag the body over to the rickshaw, and cover its face with the white cloth that signifies the dead, and tuck in the legs, out of the way of the wheels. My father would shoo the gaping, pointing street-children away. Anwar would squeeze in, beside the corpse's legs, and my father would slowly pedal down the street and into the main road, the clang-clang of his rickshaw bell resounding through the hot afternoon quiet.

I never saw Anwar complain about the work we did. He was a loyal son and he did what he was told. He seemed to have no feeling this way or that about any of it. I would have thought he would be pleased at how my father spent all that time teaching him. And how he brought him gifts: honey bananas, those small red bunches that grow only in the Nilgiris Hills, or yellow guavas from the fruit-man near the Durga temple, or fresh hot mysore pak from the next-door neighbor's sweet-shop on the main road. I would always get some too, but everyone, my mother and my father would say, Oh, let

Anwar eat, don't bother him, you know he works so hard, he's the one who needs the strength! I took to stealing from the closed plate in the main room (which was our front room and eating-room and cooking-room) at night, it was the only way I could get my hands on the sweets especially, which Anwar loved. Sometimes gulab jamun thick with rose syrup, sometimes laddus fragrant with cardamom, the falling-apart kind rich with ghee-fried raisins and cashewnuts.

I was too late sometimes. Once, after my afternoon bath, I saw him finish eating something from a dried-leaf cup. He put the cup down and went to the outside tap to wash his hands. I touched the cup, thrust my fingers into the sweet stickiness lining the leaf, licked them. It was fresh syrup from a gulab jamun from the A-One sweet-shop, my father had bought this for him, as usual. I could sense Anwar turn, look at me. I scraped some more, I licked like a dog, I kept on licking, until only the taste of leaf touched my tongue. My eyes met Anwar's across the sunlit courtyard. He did not say a word to me. I knew he had not wanted to share the sweet with me. I kicked the cup with my feet and walked away.

My father would talk to me sometimes, here, Amir, go get a pillow for your father's head, or rub my calves down with oil, pa, or go help your mother with the vessels today! But he never taught me his trade as he did with Anwar, and I knew without telling what his heart wanted, and sometimes I would lie awake at night, burning inside like a forest.

I remember so well what happened then. First came the whole week of nights when I saw Anwar wake in the middle of the night and go to the courtyard. I would roll myself up to a ball and peer through the vertical bars of the low window in our room. He walked to the middle, under the drumstick trees where the bodies usually lay, and he pulled something out from his pocket. He scraped a match on the side of a box, lit a cigarette or beedi, I couldn't see what, and he smoked in the dark like any thief, waiting to ransack the house. He was fourteen years old. He finished his cigarette and lay down, right in the middle of the courtyard where every day a body or two had lain. Sometimes he stretched his arms out wide, or

16

lifted his legs, soles up, to the sky. He twisted slowly left and right, like a yogi practicing his exercises. He crossed his arms behind his head. I don't know if he closed his eyes. I don't know if he saw the moon or clouds float like gulab jamun in the blue syrup of that midnight sky. He lay there, motionless, face turned to the heavens.

I squinted upward from the window and imagined how his thoughts, which he shared with none of us, streamed silently out and rose with the wind to merge continuously with the far and sparkling powdery river of stars. Every night he woke, for a whole week, and every night I woke when he woke and watched him. I fell asleep by the window, watching, slipping down my mat till only my head rested on the windowsill. In the morning I found him beside me in the room, steadily sleeping. My head still on the windowsill, sometimes an arm wrapped around a windowbar. I knew then he must have known I knew about his night-time waking, but he did not speak of this knowledge with me. In the daytime his face was carefully closed, a riverstone face he turned to me as to everyone else, I could not read his thinking.

The next week the cyclone they kept saying on the radio and the TV was going to hit us swept through the city, hitting us, and we had two days and two nights filled with wind and rain. Trees swayed back and forth, trees bent from the waist down like bendable straw. Branches crashed and thundered all night, you could hear only the screeching and breaking, a floated, incessant howl, like cats fighting or an infant without milk, unable to sleep. One drumstick tree in the courtyard snapped in two and fell, as if one part of it wanted to go one way and the other another. Constantly, leaves and bits of twigs from the neighbor's neem tree and the tamarinds up the street and the acacia clump by the bus stop swept like rain into the courtyard and lay in a green bed-blanket on the ground.

We were used to monsoon rain, but not wind and destruction like this. Lightning flashed continually, and it was strange, sometimes in colors, bright pink and green, Holi colors. Those two nights Anwar did not wake and go outside. He lay on his mat as if asleep, although each time I looked when the lightning flashed,

17

his eyes were open. It almost made me frightened, because his eyes were staring straight ahead, as if, where the wall was, he could see something.

Once I said something to him like, hey, Anwar, look how crazy the wind's getting, and he said, mumbling, as if he was talking to himself, you only live once. He repeated this, then he said: afterwards, you are dead.

This was the night before he vanished. Yes, it was still wind and rain all around us, in the daytime clouds so thick sometimes, branches flying in the wind, and the lightning yellow sometimes, green sometimes, when Anwar left the house. He was fourteen years old, and he did not want to do this honorable work I do, my father would say, one week later when they still could not find him, this honorable work of preparing the unassociated dead for eternity. He meant the dead who had no family, no family like ours to take care of you when you were down or who let you down when you wanted to cling to them, pass your future into their hands. But the day he left itself we knew he was gone, there was a raw blistering certainty to the storm then, that filtered to our bones. We sat on the kitchen floor tearing uselessly at our hot chapathis with our hands, unable to eat, gazing hypnotically at the small circle of flames on the kerosene stove where the rice was still cooking. My father's eyes in this light glistening with a watery sadness. Outside, the storm punished the trees, the sound of cracking wood loud in the air. The other drumstick tree was making a curious singing sound, bent nearly double to the ground.

When the rains stopped, everybody in the neighborhood looked for Anwar, even the street children, and the roast-groundnut vendor and the guava-lady and the plastic-bottle man who every day lined their carts at the end of our street, beside the Sitapet municipal school, where the bus-stop is, right next to the Durga shrine. They helped my father this way, as a matter of decency. They would expect we'd do the same if misfortune ever stopped at their doorstep. My mother came with us, sometimes, as far as the Sitapet market and the fancy-goods stores in front, she talked to herself, she was that distraught. But we did not find him. I felt foolish, because I did not expect we would. Why would he hide in the textile shops, or the liquor store, or the maidan four streets down where the rich-house boys played cricket or flew kites or sat around drinking? What street was long enough for him to lounge in, what rooftop could he possibly climb? My parents walked us in and out of the houses next to ours, tight-lipped and tight-muscled, peering into courtyards, behind zaried curtains, or up at flat roofs and terraces. I knew he had forever left us. He wanted not to be dead or to be with the dead, he wanted a life for himself. But I did not know why he had left his parents. Because it was clear to me all along they wanted him more than myself, it made me wonder what it was he hungered for, and how he could possibly have stepped away from them. I felt he must have wanted both to leave and not leave, there must have been struggle in his going.

Inside myself, too, there was a struggle, although I did not understand what I was feeling. The sadness I felt with him gone was more the sadness I imagined he must have felt, leaving, than anything else.

The time that came afterward was a silent time. My father relapsed into a stubborn melancholy, he could not laugh or joke as he had used to before, he could not bring himself to speak. He went to the mosque on Fridays as always to meet his friends, to worship, but he no longer returned calm and refreshed. My mother, who was Hindu, not Muslim like him, and had used to sing to herself in the evenings as she lit the agarbathis before her god pictures and said her prayers in the small part of the main room she had set up as her puja room, lit the two kerosene lamps very quietly and did not sing. Her pink Goddess Lakshmi floating on a calendar lotus gazed down on her without kindness. Our god, Allah, whom my brother and I had been used to visiting in mosque occasionally on Fridays with our father, seemed equally determined to be distant. No amount of kneeling to face him in the East or reciting our prayers seemed to affect him.

The work of caring for the dead had to go on (for the dead wait for no auspicious moment to arrive among us), but there was no longer instruction. The work had to be learned by me now, but now my father was not going to teach, I had to pick up what I could. I followed his hands and eyes, I did everything they did. From the beginning I felt my brother was never coming back, and I worked because I believed this was my task now, my future, and my eternity. But in my house they believed the opposite. It might be today, they would think each morning. It might be this week, or the weekend, or the coming week. I silently washed and wiped the passed-away people's bodies and did not share my belief, that it might be never, if Anwar believed he could get away with it.

The secret was in Anwar, I knew. He had held that secret close to himself. The first day of that storm, when the wind had just started muttering and heaving like an old cow in the trees, a man had come to the shade of the drumstick trees in the courtyard whose life we could not imagine. This was because no cause of death could be found for him—no knife wounds or holes in his skin, no sign of swelling or infection, no blueness like gangrene to the limbs. His face was smooth and brown and shiny like a polished coconut shell. Every part of his body gleamed like this, as if he were made of a gleaming flesh-colored metal. The look on his face was calm, not tortured, as it might have been if he had consumed poison. No snake-bites or scorpion-holes in him. The doctors were baffled, my father said, they had released him with a certificate that said Cause of Death Unknown. When you looked at his body you were mystified. He was a man who worked, he had muscle. Yet his face showed refinement—he was well-shaved, his hair cut, fingernails clean. He was like a multiple contradiction. He looked both old and young, as if his age were incidental. Everything smooth and closed into himself. Like he carried a secret all his life, and now he had died, he had taken it safe and whole away with him. The next day, after we understood Anwar was gone, this man's face kept coming back to haunt me. Once I even dreamed of him, floating in the air like a levitating yogi, closed and perfect in his sleep, under the drumstick trees.

I cannot begin to describe the way in which we lived. The days went by, the weeks, and then the months, Pongal, again, Muharram, Ramzan, Diwali, the monsoon season, the next hot season. Almost immediately it seemed the house had become a mirror of his absence. Between us a constant loss, as if the most necessary organ of the house, the live red throbbing heart, had been removed. And yet, if you can understand this, a whole year went by and we lived in the house as if Anwar was alive and lived with us.

This is how it was. There was always a plate laid out for him, and chapathis put on it, hot from the thawa, and rice, and yellow dhal with jeera. We ate as if he ate beside us even though his filled plate remained untouched. My mother filled his stainless-steel glass with water, same as always. The place behind his plate left bare, as if, any moment now, his body would fill it. After the meal my mother took his plate out, beyond the courtyard to the street, and laid it down on the ground for the street dogs. This she did every morning, every afternoon, every night, which is how a family of dogs came to live at our doorstep, and barked to guard our house at night, and wagged their tails when they saw us enter and depart. We became their sustenance. I do not know how my mother and father perceived this. They may have thought these were all ways in which they were helping Anwar, wherever he was. They were doing their part, laying out his food for him. It had become a bargain with God, a small hope that, alive, he was not ever in need, that someone, somewhere, would feed and clothe and shelter him.

And there were pomegranates still, and apples, and guavas, bought just for him. That I was still not allowed to eat, for now they would take the fruit, the day after it was bought, and give it to the poor—the beggar woman at the bus-stop or the man without legs who lived behind the Durga temple. Every now and then sweets would come to the house, but miniscule amounts—a small cone of layered soam papad from the street vendor, a single square of mysore pak, to be broken and crumbled into each of our plates, at breakfast.

And at night his mat would be unrolled, his sheet unfolded, his pillow fluffed up, a fresh glass of water laid by his pillow, in case he came back when it was dark and needed to sleep. My mother lit a kerosene lamp and kept it out in the courtyard, so he could see his way in.

I lay in the room night after night and saw the empty mat in the corner, the sheets plain and flat, pillow soft and full. I thought often of how he'd lie on his mat, hands folded behind his head, staring up at the ceiling. It was the last image in my mind before I slept. I did not think he would return. But I imagined, every night, his body in the room beside me. I felt, every night, his absence.

The days passed in a blur of routines. I concentrated on work, on helping my father with the bodies, my mother with the house. I lived the way I had always lived, and yet everything in my life was different. Inside of me I felt the hardness already setting in, smooth hardness of the muscles in the presence of death. My brother might still be alive, and yet, because he was not alive before us, he was no longer my brother. It was as if he had died and gone away, like any of the corpses who came to our drumstick tree to visit. I felt a skin begin to grow, a close leathery skin, over my feelings. It was I who had to work now for the two of us. I had to accompany my father to the hospitals first, then later in the day to the burning-grounds, where the stench of burning flesh, bleak as drying fish, fills the air for miles. Or to the Muslim cemetery where the diggers often threw me a shovel and made me dig. The days began to tumble headlong one into another, each the same as the one before, until I could no longer tell if there was any difference between sleeping and waking, working and being idle, morning and night.

But one morning I woke and without thinking started to walk down the street by myself to the local Sitapet market. It was a Sunday morning and all the shops were closed. I saw some families dressed in their church clothes heading for the Catholic church behind the Durga temple and I saw the old flower-seller threading jasmine at the corner beside the sweet-shop. I walked through the quiet streets, past the closed doors and sleeping windows, the slowly-waking people as they lined up at the street pumps with their colored plastic kodams for Corporation water, I walked past the staring slum women, the dogs sprawled in the loose debris of dustbins. I entered the market through the small alleyway by the side, near the subway and the fancy-goods store, I walked past the few slowly-opening stalls. I looked with glazed eyes at cut-open jewels of pomegranate, unruly heaps of blackening pink honey-bananas, flies already sizzling in the air above them, baskets piled with tiny white pearl onions. I took in the blue uneasy scent of sliced and bled flesh, I passed the sides and legs of goats hung upside down on iron hooks. At the masala store I smelled the high dry must of red chilies, the mountain tinder of black peppercorns. Men jostled against me, their muscles bulging and straining as they carried sacks of rice and groundnuts, going about their business. The boys helping with setting up stalls for the day, emptying boxes, arranging vegetables, paid no attention to me as I walked. I was a boy like them, and a boy unlike them, idle and wandering. Someone was playing a radio, and a woman singing Carnatic music, maybe it was Subbha Lakshmi, her voice kept going over and over the same sound—*aaahnh, aaaahnh, aaahnh*—over and over, each time a little higher. As if she were tuning in with the mridangam and veena behind her for the start of a song, just tuning in, not singing anything yet, but letting the singing go through her throat and out of it, over and over.

I do not know what I was thinking, where I was walking or where I was headed. I was moving as if something in my sleep had entered my mind and was propelling me, as if a dream were pushing me onward. On my feet were the black crossover rubber sandals my brother had used to wear, and before him, some dead person who had stopped in at our house for kindness. My father had taken the sandals to wash his feet and laid them aside under the drumstick tree and then, through some strange oversight, for he never overlooked such minute details, just forgotten them. Dressed, this person went barefoot to his Maker, and Anwar inherited the sandals.

He wore them for months, he wore them everywhere outside the house, each time he accompanied my father to the hospitals, each time he disappeared by himself, each time he rode on the rickshaw, before he discarded them. They were too large really, he said, and he went barefoot. So my father bought him soft white Bata slippers that fit better. The sandals then lay under the pile of sheets and mats in the corner of the main room until I found them one day, a full month after he was gone, and began to wear them myself. They fit loosely on my feet too, and the heel squeaked each time my weight came down on it.

Because the sandals were loose, they slipped, once, when my foot slipped on tangerine seeds and custard-apple peel and into a ragged crack in the cement poured over the pathway between the stalls. One sandal pried loose, and it is this sudden break in my steady rambling that literally pulled me up short, made me realize what I was doing, where I was, and that people I did not know surrounded me.

That night my mother once more set out Anwar's food for the night, and fed it to the mangy, flea-bitten dogs, who had started to come into the courtyard, all their tails wagging. She spoke softly to the dogs, as if they were her children. Now, now, eat slowly, she would say. Or let that one eat, what's wrong with that. She petted their heads, and their tails wagged for her. Some even licked her hands as she touched them. Once she called to me. Amir, come, get fresh water for the dogs. Later that night, after the doors were closed and the kerosene lamp taken to the middle of the courtyard and turned down low so only a smudge of gold billowed around it, I lay in my room, eyes closed and trying to sleep.

But sleep did not come to me, only the sound of the strange going-over singing I had heard that morning, transmuted. It was no longer calm and practiced, a mature singer's careful rehearsal of voice or song, it felt like it hummed beneath the ground on which we slept and started to tremble as it rose upward into the air and kept rising in pitch and volume until the sound tore like a scream through the walls and the roof and went straight upward in a burning steel flute into the starry river of sky. It felt as if the house itself was screaming, everything inside us we kept hidden, one from the other, was screaming, and only the sky, with its riven, glittering bodies shorn and distant yet forever burning, knew it.

The next day I walked away by myself again, in the middle of the day when my father was waiting outside the General Hospital by himself, and I was supposed to be waiting by the Sitapet police station, I headed in the direction of the Sitapet market but I went beyond it, toward Rampet. I walked past the St. George's boys' high school and the St. George's church and the glass bangle sellers, I walked down the street of household utensils, the rice vessels and milk vessels shining eversilver above my head, the brooms weeping upright where they stood and the new plastic dustpans sheathed safely in their plastic covers from the dirt of the street. The sun rose high in the sky. I felt the heat on my shoulders like a white-hot demon weight descending from the sky, growing larger. My shirt separated damply from the bones of my back and flapped as I walked. Tiny rivulets of sweat crept down the skin inside my shorts.

I stopped only when I came to the Shiva temple pond where they grow purple lotuses, where our mother had taken us once, to see the flowers. It felt like a long time ago. I stood on the narrow bridge linking the street to the temple, and searched through the stray violet blooms, here and there, as if I were looking for something. The temple seemed to float in a sea of large green leaves and spikes and blooms of lotus. I stared at the few intervening scoops of black water. I could not see a sign anywhere I looked. I had not known before I had been looking for one. Now I felt a gnawing achiness inside me, as if a live creature lay coiled inside my stomach and was slowly eating his way outside.

I stood on the bridge for a long time, staring at nothing in particular. Then I stared at the people coming into the temple, people sweeping the veranda, people bringing plantains for the gods, and sweet khal-khal and red kum-kum. I stared at the row of male and female flower-sellers sitting outside, weaving garlands of jasmine with their hands. I watched the boys across the street working on bicycles, blowing air into the tires, wiping the spokes with black oily cloths. I was both present to the place and absent in it. Only a part of me was standing there, foolishly watching all the activity around me, and yet this part, unconsciously arrived at this place, shielded by my own dumb confusion, felt furious and desperate to watch.

Those were my early excursions, and I began everyday to make new ones into the vast unknown that lay beyond my parents' house. I was not in school, for I was helping my father. I was not helping my father, for I was in a state of fascination with the world outside my father's house. Each day I craved a new direction, a new horizon. The smallest newness I found myself marveling at, even the sight of convent schoolgirls in their navy blue pinafore uniforms, or the sight of pinkskinned tourists in backpacks throwing bread to the ducks that lived in the Shiva temple water, among the lotuses. More and more I began to spend time away from the house, to sit for hours in various locations in the hot afternoon sun and watch other people going about their daily business. These people were alive, they had work to do, other work than cleaning the dead. Their work, I saw, catered to the living, whether rolling paan in betel leaves, cooking hot tea, tailoring saree blouses, or carrying newspapers to the offices. I sat among the rickshaw-wallas or the fruit-men with the carts, I watched them.

It was not long, only a few days, before my father noticed this distraction in me, this physical distance I was unrolling between my life and his. My mother tried to protect me, but my father got angry. You are a wastrel, he told me one day, you are not like your brother, you have not a single drop of loyalty in your blood! *I am your father,* he said, *you will do what I do, do what I tell you to!*

He began to drag me with him forcibly in the mornings to the hospitals and the police station, he no longer entrusted me alone to one or the other. But now I knew I could wander away from his side, I could watch the doctors and the nurses, the people racked with coughs or bleeding from a knife wound, stationary in the crowded Emergency Room, waiting. Or the policemen talking on their pocket intercoms, jumping onto their motorcycles.

You are becoming dreamful and useless, my father said, as he arranged a man's body in the rickshaw, sitting up, the white sheet the hospital had given draped around his face and shoulders, while

I stood by the front wheel, idly staring. Then he said it again, and I knew he was wrong about this: you are nothing like Anwar, such a good and hardworking son, you are not like your brother! He stopped and twisted his hands, as if they pained him. He himself became upset then, because Anwar's name had been invoked, and in our house, the past few months, we had stopped saying it, even though we were still feeding the dogs in his name. There was too much pain in the syllables, too much loss in the summoning of his presence. We rode home in a sullen silence. I felt as if a cloud of smoke or rain had twisted itself around my tongue. I felt unable to speak out, defend myself. But that night as I first lay alone in my bed, then got up and went to where the stars and the round shivery moon shone in the courtyard, and lay where the bodies lay during the daytime, and stretched my limbs up to the sky and, twisting, first to one side, then to the other, I knew what my father did not know yet. I saw the tiny drumstick leaves cluster around the stars, I felt the hard cement beneath my spine, and I knew already I was becoming my brother.

I was even being mistaken for him. Once, at sunset as I sat at the edge of the maidan beside the rich-people's houses with gates and gardens, watching the rich boys play cricket, a tall boy in blue jeans and a loosely open white shirt came up and sat beside me on the wooden bench. He started to smoke, offered me a cigarette. Then he took it back, as if he must have seen how young I was. He stared hard at me, then he shook his head and left. I thought you were someone else, he said. You look exactly like someone I know. I felt a chill as he walked away. I wanted to speak. I wanted to say his name. *Anwar. You knew Anwar. He was here, like I am now, you knew him.* But the boy was gone. I sat for a while longer, watching the game, feeling the fluttering of my heart as if it were a live creature inside me. It got dark and I went home, dragging my sandals in the dust. I felt I was tracing his secret life with my feet, tracing his paths, his habits.

It was a few months afterward that I left the house. It was the beginning of the monsoon season. We had already lined all our plastic buckets in the courtyard to catch the rainwater. All week we had to use plastic sheets to cover the bodies in the rickshaw, and we had to bring them inside, to the main room, to clean them. Every day we tried to ride them back, to the burning-grounds or the cemetery, but one evening it rained so hard and the water rose in the courtyard so my father said no, let us take him in the morning. The body slept with us, silent and alone in the main room, just a few feet from where I slept, as if he were one of the family. He was an old man, found dead in the gutter, beside a clutch of dead sparrows. They, the man and the birds, had all perished of food poisoning, of hotel food gone bad, a handout from the hotel. Other people who had eaten there had been rushed to the hospital. But an old beggar is easily forgotten.

I could not sleep that night. I remembered how my father cared for all the dead, as if they were his family. This man he had made a bed of blankets for, as if his body could feel the underlying softness. My mother too had lit agarbathis in the room and left a kerosene lantern by his feet, so he could see the shape of the air in the room if he so wished. As if he were her own son, sleeping for the last time in his parents' house.

I felt a warm spreading sadness for my father and my mother. They had done the best they could, they had done everything they could for Anwar and me. And it was not enough, and they did not know it. They could not make a living thing out of a dead person, they could not work for the living. They were in the hands of dead people, and this is who they were turning me over to.

I stayed awake for a long time that night. I rose from my mat once to look in on the sleeping people. The dead man lay deeply dead, my parents slept against each other, curled into themselves. My mother's gold nose-ring glinting, the specks of gray beard on my father's chin beginning to grow. In sleep they looked unguarded and peaceful.

I woke the next morning, very early, and left the house. It was dark and cloudy and raining. I put a piece of plastic over my head,

I hoisted my bag of clothes over my shoulders, and I hurried out of the house and the courtyard. A dirty white dog ran up to me in the dark, in the rain, wagging his wet bottle-brush tail, making small whining sounds with his mouth. Shush, I said to him, go away. I walked into the rain and the dog followed me. But he stopped at the end of the street, tail down, he stood looking at me, as if I were a traveler from a distant land he knew had come only to visit. I kept walking onward. Once I turned back. The dog stood, looking, a brownish white silhouette dissolving into the rain, and the whole street blurred and desolate, as if it was being washed away.

I hurried, for I knew exactly where I was going. I was going to the Shiva temple at the edge of Rampet, and beyond it, where I had seen the alleyways give way to open land and streets give way to railway lines. I was going to find the station down from those lines and I was going to board a train. I was going to go to a place I had never seen before, the next town, or a big city. I was going to find people I could live among, living people, and work from then on only for the living. Doing what I did not know, but I was going to find out.

And this is what happened, exactly how. I was half-walking, half-running, because it was still raining, and it was dark, and though the street lights were on, their yellow reflections in the pools of water in the street made the light confusing. No one was in the street but myself. No one, not a crow, a rat, a gray pigeon. Most people were asleep in their beds, intending to wake at a godly hour, and even the roosters were sleeping. But it was not daybreak yet, no light was making an appearance. The plastic over my head was not enough to cover me, water dripped and flew at me from the sides so I was wet in less than twenty minutes, water running warmly down my body. My shirt and pants were soaked and clung wetly to my skin. I came to the Shiva temple, a shroud of rain over the gopuram, I climbed the bridge in front and stared at the giant sleeping lotuses being battered by rain, the large folded leaves as they shuddered, the billowy petals. I could smell the stale used air from a thousand malais of jasmine, a thousand offerings of rose petals, a thousand overripe bananas from yesterday's puja. A damp ferment of leaves rose from the water. No one was in sight. The rain made a swishy white curtain in front of the street light and fell frothily to the ground. I turned, I hurried onward.

It was after I'd passed the closed tool shops I had never passed before, bicycle shops I had never seen, rows of tire shops and old garages, and was looking at the streets, wondering which one to try for the railway lines, when I stumbled into a doorway with a flat extended awning over it. I stood for a minute under it, wringing the water from my shirt. Then I decided to take shelter for a little while. Other people were already using this space as shelter. Two men rolled up in blankets were lying right up against the door. A fruit-vendor who had parked his cart on the cement apron in front lay curled under the cart like a dog.

I stood, watching the rain fall in long white streamers beneath the white mercury lamp across the street. It had become heavier and I shivered. It had also become a little colder. I slid down to my haunches. Then I sat in a lotus. Then I put my head against the rolled-down aluminum door, my bundle sliding down beside me, and inexplicably, for I had believed myself alert and wide-awake, I slept.

When I woke it was light and everyone was awake. The smell of fresh wet earth was strong in my nostrils. It looked like it might be about seven or eight in the morning. The rain had stopped. There were people walking about in the slowly steaming street. I looked around, pulled myself upright. The two men who had slept beside me had disappeared. The fruit-man had pushed his cart away from the door and wheeled it to the side. Now the pile of fruit covered the night before was exposed. Bright yellow and orange mangoes rose in pyramids against each other. And beside the cart, seated on a small wooden stool, eating a mango, was Anwar.

A sprouting of beard and moustache obscured the lean features I knew. His long hair curled down to his shoulders. The moment blurred, a shocked series of impressions, one after the other. Like looking at a ghost of someone you had known once, long ago, when you were both brothers in the same house, and had slept for years together, in the same room. It felt, remembering, like another life. His face still thin, eyes sunken, as if the sleep he'd had wasn't enough. But Anwar. It was Anwar.

He looked at me and bit into his mango, which he was holding in his hand so that the juice ran down his elbow and onto his shirt. My eyes traveled over him. His shirt was torn in about a hundred places and did not look like a shirt. Like a rag, rather, with holes that he had hung about his shoulders. His khaki shorts were turned black with dust. His feet were bare, and even from here, a few feet away, I could see the cracked skin on his soles climb toward his ankle.

It is telling that we did not speak in this first moment that we looked at each other and saw what the other was doing. I saw he was now a mango-man. He must have seen I was now a runaway, just like him. We observed these things for a few moments. Then he spoke.

You want a mango? He held one out to me.

I got up, walked over to take it. I did not say, that is the first time you have offered me something. Whose are they, I said.

The mango-man's, he said. I mind the cart for him in the mornings.

Was that you sleeping under the cart last night? I had seen the small curled figure and had not even imagined.

Yes. The mango-man lets me sleep with the cart. Since he doesn't need it.

I smoothed my fingers over the mango, catching the nub at the top. The mango was yellow with black sheared streaks and marks on it, as if it had been bumped about in a cart, or dropped to the ground. I tried to pull at the skin and Anwar handed me a knife. It was very quiet between us. It was as if all those months of his being gone had become walls and stood silently between us. I started to peel the rubbery skin with the knife.

How come he doesn't need it?

He has a house to go to, said Anwar. He has a family.

My eyes flicked toward him and away. His eyes were intent on the mango seed he was sucking at, he would not look at me.

I went back and sat down on the cement beside my bundle. I

dropped the skin on the cement, started to eat the mango. He threw his seed away when he was finished. He arced it across the street to the gutter. Then he washed his hands with some water he took from a plastic bottle.

After a while he said, You should eat your mango and go home.

The words stung. Who are you to talk, I said, feeling the long kept-down anger start up inside me like an all-consuming burial fire. The sweetness of the mango dripping over my hands and my clothes. Are you going home, I taunted, now that you have finished yours?

He did not rush toward me and grab me by the throat as I half-thought he would. He did not move. He said instead, as if he were reciting his arithmetic tables from his school-going so long ago, I have no home.

I did not have to think before I answered. You have a home, I shouted. You have a family! You have a father and a mother who wait for you as if there is nothing else on earth to do! You have a hundred dogs who eat the food they put out for you everyday, who are all fed in your name!

Something was twisting upward through me and choking me as I spoke. I dropped the half-eaten mango, grabbed my bundle, and started to go.

But I had just woken, I was in a strange street, I was confused. I did not know which side to go. I saw I was in the middle of a street lined with shops that stretched in both directions. I was not sure which side to walk, to find the trains. I stood, poised to run, I did not know in what direction.

Then I heard it. Anwar's face had gone still, his eyes round, then he was shouting something back to me, but I was listening to what rumbled beyond him. Over his voice a slow rolling rumble of a sound. A train sound. I listened, it came closer. It was behind Anwar, it was that side. I started to run. Anwar caught me as I went past him, lunging at me. That's not the way home, he shouted.

You go home, I shouted back, it's your turn to be the only son! I started to run then, dodging bicycles, men with carts, scooters, mopeds. Anwar came behind me, shouting my name. Amir! Amir!

All I wanted was to get away from him, the ghost he had become in my mind. I ran past the people staring, the shops, I came to an open space and now I could see, in front of me the street ending, the stretch of empty grass with rubbish strewn all over, and the railway tracks. My sandals clunked and squeaked and fell outside my feet as I ran. Anwar had abandoned the mangoes and was shrieking after me as if there was anything he could say that would turn me back. I ran, clutching my bundle. I ran, trying to remember what my plan was. To catch a train, or to find a station? To climb into a running train, or to follow the tracks somewhere?

I was in the middle of the train tracks now. The sound of that train coming was very loud in my ears. I looked up once and saw the round black engine of the train approaching. There were so many rail tracks. I tried to make out which track that train was on. The gravel piled on the tracks got into my sandals as I ran. Then my foot slipped. The sandal flew half off my foot and got wedged in a track. The other half of the sandal was wrapped firmly around my foot. I bent, struggled with it. The train very close now. I could see the black round engine, the long curved plow in front. A siren blew, and the sound was in my ears like a shuttling, disjointed scream. I tried to unloose the sandal from my foot, my foot from the sandal. I saw the frantic horror on Anwar's face as he came struggling toward me, shouting. I saw the blue washed-clean sky above, a streamer of violet cloud. I saw the black grime of the train's face. Then it was upon me.

Everything in me jolted, pushed, tumbled outward. Everything black and screeching and grinding. Many-sided the everything, many-sliding. In the second that I felt the hurtling weight knife my bones and saw, simultaneously, the bright white exploding of the death light in my face, and was tossed, shattered, whole, down into the long tunnel of my death, there was a terrible confusion in my mind. I was not sure who I was, where I was. The present and the past got confused in me. The future compressed into that moment and pushed through my skin. I could no longer reach out and feel what I wanted. I felt myself both paralyzed and moving. I could not sense where I was going. I could not make myself get up, hurry onward, as I had, just a moment ago, when I fled from Anwar. I was being pushed through something by something outside me. I was being moved, not moving myself. It was disorienting, unbelievable. It was like being pushed from a dream of another life, where you were someone else, into a cloud of fog covering your memory. No longer capable of recognizing the world.

Afterward, it seems like a very long time afterward, although it is not, that I am calm, that I understand what has happened, where I am, where I am going, why the ground appears far below me, and I can see, not merely tracks, a train, scrub around, but a spread of city, silver rail tracks winding through it, tens of thousands of houses, the tops of palms, and everywhere a stream of people, in cars, bikes, on foot, moving, moving, moving. Far away the aqua fringe of ocean, white lace at its edge, so close to the city. Just below it seems no time has passed at all. The train has stopped and people stream out of the train on either side to come to the front, where the engine and what it has collided with stand, confused in their mutual spasm. A small knot of people stand directly in front. They make no effort to come closer, to touch the body. But Anwar, who knows with his hands the feeling of death, is close. He is touching the red checked shirt, the torn black pants, the broken foot in the broken sandal. He is weeping as if it is his own brother who lies before him now, mangled and public, a corpse already. He is putting the bones inside the clothes. Covered with blood, long before the ambulance arrives, screeching its own siren down the waking streets, his hands are pulling the body out from under the wheels. While I keep on rising through the shivering velvet of cloud into the flicker of blue, and begin slowly to feel again. The tiny drops of moisture, almost jasmine-scented, of the cloud. The warm roll of sun, turning over on my face. The touch of my brother's hand, sweet as syrup on my skin, smoothing my quiet body.

What the Watchman Saw

ℒ Venkatesh had been a watchman for twenty-two years on Second Cross Street in Radhakrishna Nagar when he glanced across the street and saw a flashlight flicker in the new neighbor's house. He also heard the scuffle of feet, the muffled sound of voices, somebody swearing, and an urgent summons to a possible accomplice. *Arrai, Shankar, Shankar!* It was half past one, the night was dark, and no light shone but two of the four mercury street lights, paced evenly at fifteen-yard intervals down the street. (The other two had gone out months ago, the city had not yet replaced them.) He froze where he sat, on his gray steel folding chair outside the Dev Maharaj Villa, the humble abode of his employer Mr. Devrai, the zari saree magnate who had made a fortune out of customizing zari sarees from the South for the ever-needy North and had employed Venkatesh expressly to sit still and monitor the street for any species of threat to his own private villa, his personal property, or his person.

Not to his neighbors.

Conscious of which expectation, for a long unhappy moment, Venkatesh sat. He was a dutiful man, and although, over the years, he had come to think of himself as a benign (though essential) part of the street (alert yet invisible), he did not mean to venture outside the bounds of duty. Most often, nothing much happened. He watched the street, walked up and down, tapping his cane on the hard tar, interrogating untoward night-wanderers in the vicinity of the Dev Maharaj Villa. At night the street felt like his private terrain (no other watchman prowled its length), and so he turned his head uneasily, listening.

In the distance, lorries heaved, their diesel wheeze rocked against the sound of the gravel or steel rods they carried. Closer in, the raspy bass of the first speaker and the more nasal tones of Shankar communed. Shuffling sounds proceeded, as if things were being dropped and lifted. The Dobermans at the corner house barked.

And the light flickered again. Through the screen of crotons and decorative palms in the neighbor's garden, Venkatesh observed a wide cone of light shiver across the wall of the house's front room.

Without expressly intending to, yet propelled by a commingled sense of trepidation, curiosity, and vague protectiveness, Venkatesh slowly rose and crossed the road. Through croton leaves he caught a blurred glimpse of a blue baby Krishna on the wall, a chain of sandalwood beads pendent over a dimpled face. The light moved and the giant shadow of a hand appeared. A string of dried mango leaves across a doorway.

The light switched off. Venkatesh stood, peering over the four-foot garden wall, waiting.

Nothing happened.

Not certain what to do next, he tried to push the trellis gate open. The gate swung in. It had been left unlocked. Venkatesh paused. The smell of jasmine blew gently against him. The Dobermans barked in unceasing, resolute fashion. Venkatesh reasoned with himself. He was not exactly breaking into the neighbor's compound. In a manner of speaking he was the neighborhood watchman. Wasn't he? Venkatesh entered the garden. Hand on his stick, canvas shoes stealthy on the path, he sidled up to the window of the front room and peered in. It was dark again, and empty. But from somewhere inside the house, the sound of muffled voices continued. The sound of doors opening, people moving.

Venkatesh looked around. The garden went around the house. Bushes of ixora, hibiscus, bougainvillea thrust up under the windows. Ample coverage for a would-be burglar, peering in, or, the thought crossed his mind, for a would-be hero, spying on a burglar. Carefully, attuning himself to the sound of voices, he began to move toward the back of the house. Through windows he strained for a glimpse of what was going on. The windows were open: glass shutters pulled back, trelliswork shiny with new paint. No curtains had been hung up yet. The neighbor had moved in only a few days ago, and he had not fully moved in as yet. But all the rooms on this side of the house were clear.

Puzzled, Venkatesh kept moving. Half-crouched as he approached a window, pushing himself up against whatever bush presented itself.

Near the back of the house, he stopped. Lights were flickering again. The voices louder. He squatted into a hibiscus bush when he reached the window. This was the room. The flashlight skittered across the empty walls of this room. Thumps and swearing pummeled the air. Very carefully, lifting his head fractionally, one centimeter at a time, Venkatesh peered in over the sill.

And this is what he saw.

He saw the light play erratically on an almirah in the corner. A wooden almirah, cavernously open. Then eyes. A sudden conflagration of eyes: wooden, metal, stone hollows of eyes fixed abruptly on him. Swatches of straw and cotton padding flung across the room. Limbs, torsos, breasts. Gods. These were gods, barely three feet tall. Sprawled, seated, and upright, inside the almirah and across the room. Lakshmi on her lotus. Ganesha bending his trunk benevolently over his giant paunch. Several dancing Natarajas. A host of Krishnas, playing the flute. For a moment he felt like he was in the back room of a store or warehouse, surrounded by the figures of the deities, on sale by the dozen.

The night pressed back on his limbs and seemed to disappear. He felt disoriented, as if he were a clerk at the warehouse, rather than a night watchman peering into his neighbor's house. He looked at the three men plunging among the idols, turning them over, examining broken limbs, rubbing at dust on sleek bronze shoulders, not following.

The gods looked old and tired. In the changeling light of the flashlight they glinted their brass and copper and dark wood faces up at him. They were regular, ordinary gods—the same kind you saw at the temple and gave coconut barfi and bananas to. The same kind you found adorning hotel lobbies, rich people's houses, and tourism bureaus. You could find gods like these at any handicrafts store—such as Tamil Nadu Handicrafts or VTI. What were these fellows doing, stealing them?

One of them, a wiry barefoot fellow with a cloth around his head, was lugging a heavy stone Ganesha to a door in the back. Another in a light-colored dhoti and shirt was lifting a dark metallic boar's head, the snout gleaming black gold—the boar's head incarnation of Vishnu. The third, a heavy-built fellow with white dust in his hair, was trying to carry two gods, one under each arm—a brass representation of Saraswati, and a tall, dancing Shiva Nataraja— but Saraswati's long veena kept knocking into the gods behind her. The Nataraja had one of his four arms missing.

Rooted in the hibiscus bush, Venkatesh shook his head. These fellows were wasting time. Their time, and his time. You could buy a good god in a store in broad daylight. A whole god, limbs intact and new. Why bother stealing these decrepit ones?

For a brief moment he considered challenging them. *Nilunguh!* he could shout, pointing his stick at them. What are you doing, stealing this man's deities? But even the thought felt insipid. What could they possibly say? They might not have a coherent answer. They might mumble something about selling them to tourists. Or donating them to their village temple—as if a temple could not afford to buy its own gods or make them, out of some naturally bountiful material, wood or clay or stone. It seemed pathetic all around, this pilfering of idols.

The men emerged into the open through the back door. The Dobermans were going berserk with their barking. Other dogs, in other houses, had started to join them. Venkatesh unhinged himself from the bush and inched his way to the corner of the house.

Two more men, these two hefty, with what looked like truncheons in their hands, lurked outside, by the water pump. The party did not seem to wish to linger. In an elaborate ungainly dance, the men began to carry their spoils to the back of the yard. A wood-and-rope ladder stood propped against the six-foot wall. Like women at a construction site, climbing to different steps, they passed the gods one by one up the ladder to someone on the other side. Then, as Venkatesh watched, they completed their climb up the ladder and disappeared.

For a few minutes Venkatesh stood, feeling the hard cool wall behind him, hearing his uneven breathing while the dogs' barking tapered to a sporadic desultory protest. Here in this backyard the smell of lime, citrusy sweet, from a thorny lime tree near the back wall was strongly in the air. Beyond the wall and the next street's layer of houses, sudden car engines revved up and died away.

Later that night, back at his vigil but dozing off momentarily, Venkatesh dreamt he had tried to stop the burglars. He pounded after them, stick raised above his head, blowing his whistle, shouting at them to stop. Voices blew about him, round stone voices, high metal voices, thick clay voices. *Help*, they shouted. *Help, help!* Venkatesh tried to keep his eyes on the gods as they were carted off by the thieves, tucked under arms, wriggling and trying to escape. Their mouths were wide open, and their voices came out of their mouths in long hopeless strings of sound. *Help us*, they were saying, *help, help!*

The rest of the night seemed tame by comparison. Venkatesh walked across on occasion and peered into the neighbor's garden. But the thieves did not return. He wondered about the neighbor, who had left an almirah full of gods in an empty house and had yet to occupy it. He had seen him arrive in a van a few times, with some men. They had unloaded furniture and large cardboard boxes. Clearly of not great value for the neighbor had not even locked his gate. Nor, possibly, his back door, although the lock could have been prised open.

While the sky lightened and the tinny city stars faded, Venkatesh wondered if it was worth reporting such an innocuous crime to the local police station. They were only handicrafts. But still, they were someone's prized possession. Mulling it over, he dissuaded himself. He remembered the spread of idols across the room. Such things could not matter much. This man had so many idols he would not miss a few. And surely something he had witnessed alone, without bystanders, sensitive and censuring, could not be of much import.

Venkatesh thought this thought because by now he was used to effacing himself, to taking a secondary role before most denizens of the world. In all matters simple and complex, he had come to consider himself adjunct not central, useful not vital. Perhaps this inclination could be traced to his childhood as the middle son in a family of five, lost between siblings, often overlooked. But expected early to earn for his family (first as shoeshine boy, later as postal peon, office peon, finally night watchman), subsume personal want in the satiation of his family's wants. Perhaps it was this, the long years of working for others in menial positions, of saying *yes saar no saar* in equal measure, of keeping employers' secrets over the years, that had made his self-effacing habitual. Talking was a case in point. More often than not someone else was relaying his vision of the world, Venkatesh was responding absently with little doses of amava?s and really?s.

Nevertheless, a while later, as he surrendered his post to the day watchman and paused at the corner vandi for his morning cup of coffee, Venkatesh felt buoyant with heroic intention. He *would* go to the police, he ruminated, swirling the hot milky concoction over his tongue, explain exactly what had happened. He would mention the back door entering, the casual rummaging among the neighbor's goods. He would recall the ladder, the two thugs waiting in the back yard, the getaway cars. He would point out the overpowering number of them, clambering over the wall. As he walked to his home in Kalyani Nagar, contemplating his overgrown toenails in his old leather sandals, Venkatesh devised comprehensive answers to the paunchy police sergeant's searching questions. (The sergeant had arrived whole and minutely filled-out in his mind, down to the insignia on his khaki epaulettes and the double curl on his caterpillar moustache.) He felt certain the police would laud his coming forward, his sharp observations, his meticulous testimony. No one in the history of such incident reportage would be recalled to be as thorough, as observant. His career as watchman (though modest) would stand him in good stead as he renumerated each action in detail.

In his house, Venkatesh rolled up his khaki uniform in a bundle, took a bath, ate the hot breakfast of idlis and coconut chutney his wife put before him, then stretched himself out in his bed. The scenes of the night before played in his mind as he continued to make out his official report at the station.

It was only as he was beginning to doze off that a particular question of the sergeant's gave him pause. And what were you doing, saar, the sergeant asked, fingering his double-curled moustache in an oily way. Why didn't you stop them?

That night, Venkatesh left the house earlier than usual. He was not calm as he normally was, a watchman heading to his night's duties. He felt unusually restless and agitated.

He went down to the Mallipooh market at the corner of Second Cross Street and Fourth Main Road. He knew the apple vendor there, and the woman who sold onion and garlic, and the old man Thiruvel who roasted groundnuts. He even talked on a regular basis to some of the rickshaw pullers who slept under the neem tree just outside the market.

He stopped to chat with Thiruvel.

In less than a few minutes, rolling the hot skin of groundnuts in his hands as he peeled and popped them in his mouth, he had ascertained that none of the vendors had been aware of the break-in. His heart felt heavy, for it had been his secret hope that one of them might have witnessed the heist and could take on the onus of reportage. But of course, they were not nocturnal workers like himself. They all packed their wares and left well before midnight.

As he emerged from the market, however, a rickshaw puller

stopped him. What kind of commotion there was last night, he remarked unexpectedly. You saw what was happening, saar?

Accosted, offered this chance to distinguish himself, Venkatesh stumbled. The suddenness of the question pushing him reflexively into denial. I? Why would I see what was happening?

The dogs were barking the whole night long. It was like the dead had come alive and were walking the streets.

Venkatesh laughed, a short uneasy laugh. In the space of a breath, he had realized he could not explain looking into the neighbor's house while doing nothing to save the neighbor's house from being robbed.

Oh, dogs, he said. They are always barking!

Another rickshaw puller joined in. When a dog barks like that, it means something, he opined.

Not at all, asserted Venkatesh. Dogs bark for all sorts of reasons. Sometimes they are just practicing their barking.

Maybe something happened that we don't know about, suggested the first rickshaw puller.

The police would know, offered the other, trustingly.

A small relief washed over Venkatesh. Of course, he thought. Why hadn't he thought of that before? After all, the police station was only a few hundred yards away, on the main road. And policemen, like night watchmen, remained on duty at night.

Oh yes, he said, in echo. The police would know such things.

Yes, nodded the second puller. Somebody would have called the police if anything happened.

At this Venkatesh felt a pang of disquiet. *Except if it happened in an empty house,* he thought cogently to himself. But he did not say anything.

He took his leave and went up to the house. The day watchman was packing his lunch box and water bottle into his cloth rice bag in preparation to leave. Saar left for Coimbatore today, he said. Venkatesh nodded. He had known the Saar was going to Coimbatore, to transact some business with a textile factory owner there. The day watchman continued, Mrs. and the boys too. There's only Savithri, up at the house. Savithri, the housekeeper, had worked for

Mr. Devrai almost as long as Venkatesh had. Here, you want the newspaper? He handed the day's Indian Express out to Venkatesh, who had taken to reading the day watchman's newspaper these days. Venkatesh took it, and the day watchman mounted his bicycle and left.

An hour or so later, Venkatesh was seated on the front steps, drinking the sweet tea Savithri had made, idly rustling through the newspaper, when a dark blue van drove up to the gates of the new neighbor's house and paused, engine still running. They both turned to look.

Venkatesh recognized the van. That's the new Saar next door.

Savithri said, wonderingly, Why is it that van comes only at night?

The driver got out and opened the gates. He drove the van up the private driveway to the house. Men spilled out of the van—the new neighbor, short and stout in a checked brown shirt and loose black pants, several others, large and muscled and clad in shiny black and striped jogging clothes.

Who, said Savithri, are all these people? She stood watching them, a petite contrast in her carefully-tied maroon Tanjore cotton, her gray and white hair pulled into a knot.

Venkatesh took a gulp of hot tea. For what, you're watching them? They must have their own business to look after. He said this unconvincingly, even to himself, uncomfortably aware he was as curious as she about these proceedings. The men had opened the back of the van and were unloading boxes. Large cardboard boxes, of the kind he had seen before.

Savithri shook her head. Goondas, she said. Those people don't look like our people.

Good people, she meant. Decent, normal, good people, like us. Venkatesh could see there was something cold and efficient about the way those men were moving. He was beginning to feel unhappily she was right. House-shifting, he said, weakly. No need to call them goondas.

Not believing this himself. The size of the biceps on these men being more than a little troubling.

Someone shouted, from inside the house. The men looked at each other, then dropped their boxes and rushed into the house. Venkatesh hurriedly drank the rest of his tea and handed the ever-silver tumbler to Savithri. For some inchoate reason he wanted her to be safe inside when the neighbor discovered the horror of the robbery—which discovery appeared to be under way currently.

But he didn't have to worry. Oblivious to high drama next door, Savithri had turned her attention elsewhere. I can't spend all night talking, I have to go finish the sambar, she said brusquely as she went inside.

Venkatesh cautiously returned to his seat outside the Dev Maharaj villa. He sat quietly, listening to the continuing sound of shouting from inside the neighbor's house. Then he opened his newspaper and perused the headlines. He started to read about the day's suicide bombings in Iraq, the killing of children in a refugee camp in Palestine. The news made him tremble. He sat, holding the newspaper, traveling involuntarily to Iraq, to Palestine, to murder-stricken Sudan, as the words resolved and entered him. His hands shook.

After a minute he realized someone had walked over to his chair and was standing above him. With a start he looked up. A mustard checked shirt drawn tight across a thrusting paunch met his glance. A triangle of chest hair, a thick gold chain tangled in it. Oily black hair that curled down from a bald spot and rested on a mustard collar. What looked suspiciously like a diamond earring glittering from an ear. Foggily, Venkatesh realized who it was. It was the new neighbor.

Uh hello saar, he attempted.

You work here? asked the neighbor. His voice peremptory, like a judge's, or a policeman's, or a headmaster's.

Venkatesh fumbled. Aama, saar.

You're the watchman?

I am the night watchman saar for Mr. Devrai.

Then you would see what happens on the street at night?

I guard Mr. Devrai's house saar.

Yes yes, said the neighbor, sounding impatient. But this week did you see anything in my house at night? That house, across the street. That house I own. He pointed.

And here it was: the ultimate opportunity to redeem himself. The moment of truth, prompted.

And once more Venkatesh found himself unable to speak it. He found himself afraid instead to confess his inaction to this man, the man himself whose house was robbed. He met the man's probing eyes, despairing. It was not purely the fear of being considered inept. Or incompetent. It was a horrible form of inertia that held him now in its grasp. So unwittingly had he started on this route to deception, so mired was he that he could not veer away.

No, no, saar, he said unhappily, while guiltily conscious he needed to push the pretense further to be credible. I didn't see anything. Why saar, what is wrong?

What is wrong! Someone broke into my house when I was gone, that's what is wrong!

Broke in ah?

Yes, broke in! Robbers got into my house and you say you saw nothing?

No saar. Venkatesh made a supreme effort. Why saar, did they take something?

They stole—the neighbor stopped himself. From the bottom of his discomfort, a thought floated up into Venkatesh's head. The man looked disproportionately agitated for the loss of a few handicrafts. They stole some very valuable things, said the neighbor, sounding desperate.

Jewelry? asked Venkatesh, striving to act normal and unknowing.

Yes, jewelry! These things cannot be replaced!

This gave Venkatesh brief (though not terminal) pause. Now two of us are lying, he marveled. These things are strange indeed. You went to the police saar? he inquired.

No no, said the neighbor, irritably, there's no need for the police!

The police station is just on Main Road, saar, near the bus stop.

What, you didn't hear me? No need for the police, I said. The neighbor was fixing Venkatesh with a penetrating glare.

Venkatesh, whose sweat was already beading and sticking to the inside of his shirt, began to feel more uneasy at this. No no saar, he agreed, not certain anymore what exactly he was agreeing to.

I settle my affairs myself, said the neighbor, meaningfully.

Ah yes yes saar, murmured Venkatesh. He searched in his back pocket for his handkerchief. Sweat had formed droplets on his forehead.

How long have you worked here, asked the neighbor, in a sudden conversational tone.

Many years saar. Venkatesh mopped his forehead. Almost twenty-five years.

You have a wife, a family?

Oh yes saar. Two sons and a daughter. Very good family saar. A part of him was faintly relieved the conversation had turned to milder seas, but a part of him bobbed about in dull confusion. Why focus on his situation now?

You take care of your family?

Oh yes saar.

You wouldn't want anything to happen to your family? The note of distinct and uncalled-for menace with which the neighbor now leaned over Venkatesh was not lost on Venkatesh. Under the man's piercing stare, he fumbled. No no saar.

You would do your job well so your family was safe and happy?

Oh yes saar. Venkatesh heard his voice become fainter, as of a man disappearing inside a well.

You would notice if burglars came into the house next door to steal things?

Oh yes yes saar.

Then what did you see?

Now Venkatesh felt disheveled, as if he had fallen into a ditch and snagged his clothing on a thornbush, and lost his foothold to dung or mud. No no, saar, he said. Nothing, I didn't see anything saar.

At this moment, somebody called hoarsely from across the street and the neighbor looked up. The goondas, or house-shifters, were gelling in a cluster by the gate. One of them beckoned, his motions frantic. *Saar saar*, he was shouting. Something else has gone, *saar!* The neighbor looked down at Venkatesh. I'm going now, he said. But I'll be back!

Venkatesh said nothing. He watched as the neighbor crossed the street and the group re-entered the house.

The night was no longer quiet about him. Two moths had alighted on his portable kerosene lantern, buzzing as jarringly as giant electric saws. The lantern itself seemed to be transmitting waves of an audible frequency. Inside his chest, his heart was beating a rapid staccato like a rudely urgent hammer, he could not quiet it.

A few hours later Venkatesh received his second shock of the evening.

The men next door had returned to their shifting and carrying. Venkatesh watched in trepidation. But after a while they locked up the house and left. Venkatesh kept his eye on the men as they climbed into the blue van. He said a prayer of thanks in his head to Hanuman, the god of rescues and sudden salvation.

The van reversed into the street and drove away.

Left with his newspaper, Venkatesh opened up to the inner pages bristling with domestic and national news. An Indian man living in the United States had cut up his wife and put her in a suitcase. Two women in a local Home for the Aged had adopted a family of bats who resided with them in the Home's topmost room. Border patrols on the Rajasthan border reported firing from the Pakistani side. In retaliation, the prime minister had informed Musharref that India was in the possession of more nuclear weapons which had not yet been test-detonated. Ancient statues had been stolen from a temple near Tanjore.

Venkatesh stopped, mainly because there was a picture beside this last story. A tall, three-armed Nataraja looked unsmilingly back at him. It was not clear from the picture whether the fourth arm had been removed or was intentionally missing. Bronze, locked in the circular intimacy of a pronged universe, the Shiva looked inscrutable and grainy.

A little confounded, Venkatesh began to read the story. After Operation Blackhole, he read, when Indian police had arrested Indian billionaire Vaman Ghiya, the artful art collector, for stealing and selling ancient statues and friezes of the gods from temples all over India to foreign buyers, often eventually to Sotheby's, the famous auction house in New York, possibly with the surreptitious involvement of Sotheby's itself, police were cracking down twice as hard on other suspected stealers of ancient art. And this species apparently abounded. There was still a healthy trade in such art around the world. Antiquities, they were called. The law in India was that no statue more than a hundred years old could be exported, let alone traded for profit. Yet tenth- and twelfth-century statues were turning up in Christie's, in Sotheby's, in European and American museums. It was suspected, he read, that art dealers worked under the table with art collectors abroad, arranging beforehand, as Ghiya had, to steal selected pieces of art. Common thieves were in cahoots with wealthy collectors. Auctioneers, middlemen, and traders got away scot-free. Ancient deities, some dating from the BCs, disappeared forever.

The three-armed Shiva Nataraja, he read, was unique and precious, a one-of-a-kind deity. No one could tell if the three-armedness had been intended or accidental, although a slight knobbed swelling on the shoulder seemed to hint at a once-existent former arm. What was known was that the Shiva dated from the seventh century AD and was now MIA, along with a clutch of other deities— a Saraswathi among them, and several Lakshmis, and a motley selection of Krishnas and Hanumans. They had all been resident at a barely known temple near Tanjore. Although ancient, they had been worshiped everyday. Pujas were offered daily to them, prasadam laid at their feet and offered to devotees. At festivals they had been washed in milk. Often they were clad in silks. Now overnight they had vanished.

Venkatesh read the article again, just to be sure. The words on the page seemed to have metamorphosed into prickly caterpillars intent on crawling over the hairs on his arm.

The words seemed to be saying something preposterous.

In short, they were saying the new neighbor was an art thief. They were adding two and two in his head and coming up with a nearly four. The nightly arrivals, the van unloaded, the sheathed cardboard boxes. Then the empty house, the almirahs seething with gods and goddesses, many of them misshapen and dilapidated. Scarcely fresh and new, as any respectable collection of handicrafts might be expected to be. Yet deities seductive to other nighttime prowlers, intent on break-ins. The irrefutable theft of the three-armed Nataraja, its presence and its removal. Finally, the peculiar menace directed at himself. Unhappily, these things added up. Like Vaman Ghiya, the new neighbor, it was possible, was a stealer of antiquities. The thought was preposterous. Venkatesh could not believe it.

He imagined telling someone, anyone this thought. He imagined the disbelief, the sarcasm, the glossing-over. Arrai, you are dreaming, pa. That kind of thing happens only in the films. Since when did you think you're a hero in a Tamil movie? Venkatesh, who was used to being disbelieved when he spoke to his superiors, to not being listened to by his peers, frowned unhappily. At midnight he sat in the pithy yellow light of his hurricane lantern, alternately toying with the thought and disbelieving himself.

Early the next morning it rained. A light drizzle, sky billowy with cloud. Wind blew leaves about. Venkatesh retreated into the compound to sit inside the small shed by the gate. Savithri came out with a broom to sweep the leaves from the front garden and the driveway.

Before the first parrots screeched overhead, the new neighbor's van pulled up by the gate and the new neighbor got out. Venkatesh, feeling uneasy, looked at Savithri's broom, how it moved in arcs, back and forth, scraping the ground, gathering up bits of gulmohar leaves, neem leaves, mango leaves, and tried to formulate what he would do or say if the new neighbor came over to speak to him.

The new neighbor crossed the street and pushed against their gate as if he lived there. Savithri stopped sweeping and stared. Yenna, saar, she said, Saar is not here.

That's alright, said the neighbor, heading toward Venkatesh.

Yenna, saar, said Savithri, obviously taken aback by the man's temerity, who do you want?

You do your work, said the man, beckoning Venkatesh out of his seat with his hand.

Good morning saar? tried Venkatesh.

You tell me, said the new neighbor, getting straight to the point, what you saw.

What saar? What are you saying? Sweat had started to break out all over Venkatesh's body.

I am saying you are a watchman, said the new neighbor, leaning close to Venkatesh. The skin on his face was oily and plump. Your job is to watch this street!

Venkatesh felt a glimmer of light open about him. No saar, he corrected, I watch Mr. Devrai's house.

The new neighbor did not seem to hear. There is something you saw, he said. There is something you heard. In the middle of the night! What did you see?

Savithri had come closer and was staring at the new neighbor. What has happened?

The man ignored her. Some men you saw, suggested the new neighbor. Some car or van you saw. Some group of men jumping over the wall!

Savithri put a hand to her mouth.

No saar. Venkatesh mustered up all his years of practice as a meek and mild watchman to project puzzlement. I already told you saar.

I know what you told me. The man inched closer.

Luckily for Venkatesh, Savithri intervened. Somebody stole something from your house saar?

You don't worry about this!

Yenna, what could they have stolen?

My goods they have stolen, said the new neighbor

What goods? Savithri had her own vast grapevine she could reach with information. She leaned forward with her broom, like a reporter.

My goods, said the man. My goods, for my business!

Aama, what business, saar?

Venkatesh was not sure why the man was answering Savithri at all. But a moment later this became clear.

Handicrafts, the man said, I sell handicrafts to the tourists!

Savithri looked disappointed. For a moment there it had sounded promising. Sound system and television, she had been prepared for. Gold jewelry and silverware would have been satisfying. She thought of lanterns made of paper and bookends in carved wood and tried to nod, reassuringly. What an outrage, she murmured, shaking out her broom.

Unlike Venkatesh, she did not suggest contacting the police. You ask Venkatesh, saar, she said instead, he is here only all night, he sees everything!

The neighbor smiled a slow snakelike smile. That is why I am here, he said, asking him!

Venkatesh wiped his sweaty forehead with his fingers. He didn't know what to say.

You describe these men to me, directed the neighbor. Tell me what they looked like!

What men saar?

You tell me what kind of car it was! Maybe you wrote down the plate number?

Savithri had resumed her sweeping. Luckily for Venkatesh, the day watchman rode up the driveway just then, on his bicycle.

Venkatesh put his things together. I am going saar, he attempted. You ask the day watchman, maybe he saw something!

The new neighbor turned to look at the day watchman, who was closing the gate. A small look of doubt had crept onto his face.

But as Venkatesh turned to leave, he said, Watchman, wait!

Yes saar?

I want you to watch my house, said the new neighbor. Until my own watchman comes to work here, I want you every night to watch my house!

Very quickly the answer to this presented itself. I cannot watch two houses saar, at once. Mr. Devrai would not like it!

Ah you do not need to tell Mr. Devrai! The new neighbor put a hand to his pocket, pulled it out, and pressed a rolled wad of notes into Venkatesh's hand.

The sweat in his palms immediately dampened it. Venkatesh opened his palm, looked down in disbelief. Five-hundred rupee notes stared back at him. No saar, he said instinctively, handing the money back. No saar! You talk to Mr. Devrai!

At this moment the day watchman reached them. The new neighbor did not push the money back on him. Venkatesh, noting he was safe while the day watchman was in sight, mumbled a hurried goodbye and almost ran to the gate. I'll come in the evening, he shouted over his shoulder to Savithri, who was calling to him from her sweeping. He shut the gate behind him and propelled himself at a stumbling run down the street.

Something was wrong. It was worse than he had thought. He turned the corner onto the main road and kept his pace up, passing the vandi where he usually had his morning coffee, not looking up as he passed the entrance to the market.

This man was worse than he had thought. Not only was he threatening him, he was trying to buy his silence. Venkatesh stumbled over a piece of stone in the road and righted himself. There was no doubt in his mind about the new neighbor now. The man was a thief, with money to roll into watchmen's hands when their Saars weren't looking. Big money. That kind of money usually meant worse. Guns, thought Venkatesh despairingly. The Tamil movies, the Hindi movies, the English movies—all pointed in this direction. Kidnappings, ransoms, threats to the family.

Venkatesh passed the police station and felt his heart beat in his chest like a jungle drum. Go to the police, the beat was saying, go to the police Now!

Tossing and turning on his bed at noon, Venkatesh tried to envision entering the police station compound. He could see the sergeant rising to meet him. He could see the long handlebars on the sergeant's mustache quiver encouragingly. He could even see, through the corner of his eye, the crowd of young recruits listening open-mouthed as Venkatesh recounted the saga of the nocturnal robbery, the planned getaway. But just as the sergeant began to press him for the houseowner's name and the house's address, the face of the new neighbor loomed dully into his field of view. *What did you say, watchman,* the face said. *Who did you tell?*

Telling the police was out of the question, thought Venkatesh.

I can have that nice family of yours removed anytime, the face was saying. I can make them vanish and never return.

What can I do, he asked himself. Night and day, this man is going to harass me?

What did you see, the face was asking. Tell me, watchman, what did you see?

What if he caved in and said he saw something? What if he stumbled and told the truth? What would happen to him, to his family?

Venkatesh slept and woke, slept and woke. At two in the afternoon, heat clammy on him like a lizard's skin, he woke to a voice, hoarse and guttural in his ear. I will get the truth out of you, the voice was saying. I will wrench the truth out of you in your sleep. You are safe nowhere, watchman! I will finish you off and your family too.

Venkatesh put a hand to his head and felt the sweat there, caking his hair like a baby's. He reached for his bedsheet and wiped his head. On the neem tree outside his window a raven was uttering a raucous sermon. I have to sleep, he thought to himself.

But he couldn't.

In the evening his legs felt like rubber, melted and flowing. He swung them over the side of the jute cot and tried to stand. It was very hot. He had barely slept. The room swayed about him. He reached a hand to the wall, leaned for a moment. His wife came into the room and found him standing there, sweating and standing.

Are you sick, she wanted to know. Are you having a chill, is it fever?

No, no. Venkatesh motioned feebly and tried to wave her away.

She left, a troubled look on her face. She came back a few minutes later with hot tea, a cut lime, cold water. She squeezed the lime into the water and made him drink. Then the tea, she said. It is a way of fooling the body, to wake it up in a minute. First cold, then hot. That way the body is strengthened. Cool down, then sweat off the impurities.

Venkatesh heard her through a rising mist of anxiety. He didn't want to be awake, and he didn't want to go to work. But his wife was already talking about his dinner, which she had made and kept ready for him in the kitchen.

Eat, she said, each time he put his hand down from his mouth. Eat, you'll feel better!

He ate a little rice and parripu, a little beans, a little mango pickle. He drank water.

As he walked to Mr. Devrai's house, he put his big men's handkerchief to his forehead and wiped. Sweat slicked off his skin and dampened the handkerchief.

Intimate scenarios of what might transpire as he approached the police station circled around him.

In one he slowed his steps to a crawl. At the gate he stepped in. A few policemen standing about looked at him idly. He ignored them and went straight to the desk where a young woman policeman sat. Her hair was plaited and lifted up into a bun. Yes, she said, what do you want?

I am a night watchman, said Venkatesh.

The woman looked at him with some respect. Yes sir?

I am here to report a crime.

That was all. It was simple as that. The woman took down his name and address. Then the name and address of Mr. Devrai. Then the name and address of the new neighbor.

Venkatesh stopped walking. He had reached the new neighbor's house. He did not know the name of the new neighbor. Outside the gate, the blue van was parked. A man in black striped jogging pants and a shiny black and silver blazer was sitting on a steel folding chair outside the gate. His hair was uncombed and long. Venkatesh recognized him as one of the goondas who had carried boxes in two days ago. The man gave him a hard assessing look as he walked by. Venkatesh made a slight gesture of acknowledgment with his hand, but it was not reciprocated. Unsteadily, he walked up to Mr. Devrai's house.

The day watchman gave him the day's news. The whole day, he said, they have been putting bars across the windows and doors.

Venkatesh looked across. It was true, thick iron bars had been laid horizontally across the shutters and bolted into the concrete at the front windows and door.

He took the newspaper and looked at it. The men who had stolen the Tanjore temple antiquities were still at large. (Miscreants At Large.) It was surmised the statues had been brought to Madras or Cochin. From there it was possible they would be shipped away to the Gulf or Singapore or Jakarta. They would swirl into the underground black market for antiquities in Europe. They would fetch the thieves huge, unfathomable sums of money. For our gods, the article said. Money paid for our temple gods. Our ancient culture pilfered like this. Pilfered and sold. Ravaged in this fashion, marketed and tawdried. People needed to come forward, the paper admonished. Rickshaw pullers, temple priests, vendors of Bisleri and Aquafina and Fanta who plied their wares by the temple gates. The police were looking for tips. It was for want of these tiny accidental bits of information that our ancient culture was falling through the cracks instead of being saved for future generations. Sometimes just one tip or two could bring an idol-robber in.

Venkatesh looked up from the newspaper and saw the goonda's eyes on his. He picked up his stick and began to walk. He would walk to the end of the street and back once, he thought. Then the second time he would walk to the end of the street and turn the corner and run to the police station.

It would take him only a few minutes to deliver his tip.

His fingers trembling on his stick, Venkatesh walked.

It was not long before dusk purpled to dark on the street. The two operative street lights buzzed and flickered and came on. Blue morning glory on Mr. Devrai's walls glowed as if fluorescent. Soon the smell of jasmine from the creepers in the new neighbor's garden wafted into Venkatesh's lungs. Mirji bhajis frying in the bhaji man's cart at the end of the street released a simmer of chili and tamarind and besan flour frying.

Venkatesh hit his stick on the ground as he walked, as a gurkha does.

For a while the goonda watched him, then he put his iPod on and started to tap his feet to whatever music he was hearing.

Venkatesh walked slowly and methodically. Each time he reached the end of the street he looked into the cave of the distance. A few vendors pushed carts, a woman crosslegged on the pavement was selling malais of chrysanthemum and sweetleaves and jasmine. The lights of Mallipooh Market shone ahead. Everything was filling out in his head now. He was no longer rubbery and uncertain. He was resolved and determined. There was just one thing left. He needed to find an entrance, a path, a way to complete his mission. He paused a few moments. Then he walked back. His stick made a predictable sound each time, and soon he was walking to a tangible rhythm.

Room Enough for the Sky

◌ She came into the room where the bird was and to the window where the light surged in, blue and full of the tearing brilliance of sky. She could see how the sky was coming apart, in shreds, like the paper (great lucent handfuls of blue handmade paper, coarse and rough, mingled with straw and mud and the raw stems of kadambaram and bark) stored here for private sale in piles around the room. Extra sheets from the cottage paper factory her husband worked at, just outside Madras, peeled and pressed in a bitterness of teal and shadow, hand-pressed, released into a sheer and grainy cellulose and dyed that stinging blue, making the room dark with their color. Outside the sky was tearing its brittle hands apart, unwieldy as cardboard, and the air full of a shredding hissing sound like snakes turning around themselves, finding the same echo of skin coiled around them—sky unceasing, pouring like liquid storm from the sky, thick with cirrus. And the churning light—such leap and ricochet of light, dangling from rooftops and trickling from windows, light flailing from roofs and the steaming surfaces of streets, calling its bodies forth as if it had language.

She stood for a second at the door because the window was moving, the two glass and wood shutters were blowing inward, propelled, it seemed, by an enormous force, the sky bursting with such intensity, bleeding its blueness into the room like ink, or raucous, uncontrollable weather, and the bird fluttered in that blueness, white wings held above, lifted, surrendered. *I am not the same voice going over and over myself,* she was thinking, *not the same window closed without volition upon itself so that every word is an echo and a memory, and nothing, not even the tendril of wind or day seeping under the door's miniscule crack could lay hold of my language, I am not imagining my own existence.*

The wind blew into the room and she saw how outside the house everything was flying, pots of cactus from the neighbor's balcony, the great fig tree from the side-yard, clothes like flying bodies from every clothes-line in the city, and slowly, the dreams. The small, restless dreams of the milk-woman, rustling, uneasy desires of the awkward fourteen-year-old boy who brought the newspaper, jangling, shimmering dreams of the street-children, and the rabid guilt of the old pimp she knew hung out at the corner of their street closer to Madras Central Station and sold every street-woman he knew into the underworld slavery that raised its stricken head at every corner and wept. She saw how everything was lifting, untethered from its moorings, even the milk the milk-woman brought every evening to the woman with the six children in the apartment across the street, small aluminum can of milk slowly overturning, spilling its white effusion over the rooftops, the dreams, the blue and shredding sky.

She was afraid for a moment and rooted as it were to the doorway until the bird's lifting, glistening wings reassured her. She rushed to him, holding her hands out, and the bird slid his velvet wings into her palms, rasp and shiver of his feathers startling and fervent against her skin. The room filled with the peculiar light of the tearing, breaking-open sky, a cool awakening indigo. She stood still. She could feel the bird's warm heart beating in her hands like creation.

In her womb, high above the bones and strings of her pelvic cage lay her own child.

Resting, she had told herself, her child was resting against the terrible burden of the world, and when it came time, the child would come forth, pouring itself down the dark tunnel of its birthing and give itself over as she had, without choice or will, to existence. She could feel in the warm caves and depths of her body a terrible questing, a reaching, as if the child coiled and inchoate inside her were awake and full of knowledge, reaching into the shimmering light of this room with its sky ripping apart in such violence and its white bird of quiet on the windowsill.

She smoothed the bird down with her hands and saw how the white of his wings was speckled and painted with gray, shadows of emerald, flickers of rust and orange. The two hearts inside her were beating, loud and dim, in a terrible cacophony of vibration that rippled along her bones and rubbed the outside of her flesh with their raw indecipherable staccato.

She was alone, she'd thought. The house empty all evening. Five stories up, and the wood paneling dark and quiet, muttering to itself with its takings in and lettings out of daylight and heat, voices of the day lodged firmly in its leaves and peelings of old, assorted wood. But she was not imagining the voice calling to her from below, the dark staircase rattling with its own unwieldy echo, *Tasneem, Tasneem!*

In her body, in the shape and posture her limbs had acquired, lay ready and waiting always that singular pulse, child's leap into obedience drummed into her cells like rain, inexorable rain that fell from the beginning of time on all the senses long ground into a single gelatinous awareness, mind quelled into a miasma of reticence, whole body turned into a will not her own, never her own, but that sprang from her, uniform and involuntary. She could hear, now, that terrible drumming along the muscles of her calf and thigh, willing her limbs to action, feel the harsh scraping of it along the chords of her throat, struggling to rise out of her mouth in irrepressible surrender, the heat of it rose in her like a flood and stained her cheeks a throbbing brown, stood out on her skin like fire. But she stood still, hardly knowing what she was doing, holding her warm, uneven breath sharply inside her, clutching at the ravaged sky with her eyes, gentian dregs still pouring like oil and torn water through the window.

Her father was dead. She had held the telegram in her hands, all morning, the pink paper of it crushed and sweating in her hands, black print bleeding into her skin, faded type of the words still rising in her mind like smoke that must rise and rise again into the smog of the city sky, thin and acrid, before it reveals itself, ribbon and trail of sinuous burning wood, and now it lay by the door where it had fallen in her rush toward the bird, a small crumpled ball of paper still emitting trickles of smoke. She could hear his voice in the small crowded apartment of their growing-up, her father bending over her mother squatting on the floor in front of the kerosene stove, kitchen thick with heat as her mother rolled chapathis and turned them one after another on the sizzling hot thawa, stove sending its flickers and tremblings of heat in an arc of rippling smoke around the room. And the children crowding into the kitchen, cutting vegetables, cleaning the meat, picking the stones from the rice, all of them, Tasneem, the youngest of the girls, and Shaheen, Farnaaz, Saira, all of them except the boys, Abdul and Farik and little Ishtar, who played outside in the streets with the neighborhood children even after dark, the girls stumbling a little, making wide circles around their father, the man with the hard voice whose house this was, whose searching eyes and swinging hands compelled yet repelled them with a terrible intensity.

They knew, because they had been told, *it was always their fault*, whatever went wrong, whatever was not on time or was askew, the chapathis burnt, dhal uncooked, they were the girls, the ones entrusted, they knew because every morning they put their burkahs on, over their school uniforms, and adjusted the small rectangular slit over their eyes, and pulled it down till it swept the cotton socks at the bones of their ankles, and hurried to the bus stop with their bags weighing their shoulders down. All the eyes of the people on their tiny covered bodies, the little children covered in black and hurrying to school, the Hindus and the Christians looking askance at them and whispering "the poor children." It was their fault

because they were female and there were so many of them, they
were the burden, the knot and the rope tied around the hands and
eyes of their parents who could no longer live comfortable lives but
must slave to house them, protect them, marry them.

And marriage came soon enough to claim them.

Farnaaz was the first to leave, even though she wasn't the eldest,
at fourteen, before she had finished school, because she was beautiful, and there were men in their father's village in the South who
offered to marry her before she turned eleven, and the man whom
her father gave her to was rich, and paid almost entirely for the
wedding. And for the clothes, all the silk sarees and cloth for the
other women in their father's life, his two other wives who lived in
the village, whom the children stared at unashamedly all through
the wedding, both in awe and disbelief, because their mother had
tried so hard to keep this secret. Tasneem was married the latest, at
sixteen, because she had shown some promise in school, and the
teachers had dissuaded her father from taking her away, they said
each time "she is brilliant, brilliant," when he came, unwilling, but
pressed and formal, in his long silk suit to the compulsory parent-
teacher meetings the school held, "you must send her to college."

If a word could be found for her father, she thought, it was negation, denial, the single terrible *no* crashing like a wild animal
through the trembling forest of their desires, their tenuous inex-
pressible desires, shrinking as he approached, insects under the
hooves, they died without a struggle. No new clothes, no pants, no
shirts, no going anywhere without the burkah, not even to the cor-
ner-store to buy chikky, no English in the house, no coming late,
not the girls, not even for the school play or Sports day, no eating
at a friend's house, no asking for anything, no shirking the cooking or the cleaning or the getting married, no asking questions,
no, no, no, a thousand times, *no.* The voices lodged deep inside the
throats, the hands folded upon themselves.

But Tasneem had dreamed of that, college, even though she
knew it would not happen, no, they knew where their lives were
going, the knowledge lodged like a cool dark stone in their throats,
yet she let herself dream, one day, of going to college, not wearing

a burkah but walking into the morass of eyes at their doorstep with her body held before her like a spear. But it had never happened, her voice was taken from her, her two eyes that saw how the world dissolved and spun endlessly around itself—weaving its own treachery, its own intrigue and naming it the holy name of tradition—her eyes were closed against herself, her body subverted, trained by the years of listening and response, years of leaping at the sound of a male voice in the house, *you must listen, must listen to your father, brother, husband, son,* the holy echo resonating like the dark rasping of wings in a cave, her body, bathed in rose-water and sandalwood, covered in turmeric and brushed to an ocher gleam, painted and patterned in the copper coils of henna, wound in the heavy silk of startling, fluorescent pink with its loud border of zari and hanging tassels, taken from her and settled into the lotus of the bridal pose in a room full of hungry, grasping women, feeling the gold chains around her neck, touching her skin, wiping her caked and powdered face, her head held down, mye-rimmed eyes held down, her voice stilled forever like the death of small birds in her throat.

It was the boy, he must have come home early, she could hear his footsteps on the stairs now, and the muscles of her stomach tightened fiercely, because she was afraid, and she knew she would see again that raw lick of desire in his eyes, her husband's brother, her own age, filled with such stems and pits of innocence in her husband's presence, who had begun to look at the blossoming contours of her body with unashamed interest. She was afraid to be alone with him, and her hand shivered a little so the bird sensed that ripple of uneasiness on his wings and jerked a little, quivering, wind brushing his feathers into a frightened halo around him.

Tasneem looked down and saw how the bird moved and how the jump of it felt like power in her hands, power of his weight rushing upward, bone and muscle and heart pulsing upward in an instinctive shudder of protest. His eyes met hers and she thought for a moment she had touched some elemental part of herself because now she could see the world unfolding in front of her, the

skin of her existence splitting apart and that other place of longing she would never acknowledge to herself existed coming toward
her, blue and lit with streaks of lightning, power of it surging into
the room like electricity. His eyes were so white, the iris white
and ringed with gray, small feathers of blue and gray like ash and
mountain water churned, swung wide around the dark cave of the
pupil.

Outside, the sounds of the blowing had grown until the whole
attic had filled with them, a thousand voices of dream breaking the
silence of sky and thrusting their breathless hands into the lit fab-
ric of air, climbing onto the wooden balconies and the unpainted
brick walls of the houses and apartments and office buildings far
in the distance. Lifting out of the black depths of the nightmare
ocean of the kitchen and the pendulum voices of *father brother husband son* and the cloistering breath of the burkah and attar of roses
poured into the bitter receptacle of quiescent skin, still encrusted
with weed and bits of shell, smell of ocean in their breath. The sky,
pulled out of itself and pouring its blue effluvium over the world
was shattering the glass in the windows, and she could hear it
crash, the splintering inward, glass flailing and desperate, brilliant
in the sun, the tinkling, the shudder, the resonance.

Nothing, she had said, when her husband came into the room, that
night of her wedding, *nothing*, when he had said, *well, is there something you want*, and she had said, *no, there's not anything, nothing
at all*, and the laugh that rose out of him snuffed the light hanging
from the bulb in the ceiling—*there is something I want, you know*,
and the world she had known collapsed onto itself.

Later she picked long green beans with her fingers, the next day
in the market, with the silk burkah sewn tight around her face and
the long stems of her fingers still rich with mehendi so everyone
knew who she was, what had happened, and they looked at her,
her bent head, her trembling hands, and said nothing. Nothing in
the world had prepared her for the tearing thrust of him deep into
the muscle of her innermost flesh, the blood stung out of her and
spilling, powerless, on the sheets, and the pain of the long-closed

entranceway torn aggressively open, compelled past its limits of extension into a Mecca of pain, no prayers to the east five times a day on her mat now helping her, no Allah descending from the heavens to tear the great weight of Muhammad Ibrahim Akbar off her chest, his heavy hands from her mouth, so that the screams were forever silenced and the heave and lust of his flesh tore deep lacerations into hers.

No one spoke about it, not even her sisters, the whispering she heard in the inner rooms became a way of saying *this is our portion*, after a while she stopped listening. It was a darkness at first that threw its thick silk and covering over her head and threatened to keep the breath from her, the sharp exquisite oxygen of survival. For days later, she thought, without knowing she was thinking, of sharp edges, thin ends of broken glass, thick serrated edges of metal knives, and rust clustering at the tips of her steel eyebrow tweezers, she thought of redness, the miracle of existence bleeding out of her in a violence of desire, she thought of death as if it were morning, a sudden coming into a legacy of air. But then it faded, the dark turned sallow and restless, coal burnt by inexorable time out of its own existence into ash, a struggling heap of powder, edges blunted and dimmed, the blood ceased abruptly, spreading its felt into every corner of the dim house until she could feel its throb as the taste of dust in her mouth, and no more.

What she carried in her was growing. In that limbo in which she moved, the child became a part and extension of the gray dissolution. Now and then she felt him knocking on the doors of tissue and blood he lay against, mute and questing, stretching his restless fingers against the sanguine web that held him in, and she wished she could avoid the descent, the expulsion to come, wished she could hold him inside her forever.

One day, at about seven and a half months, when the drumstick was flowering, she had ventured outside, down the long narrow stairs and into the backyard where the drumstick grew, thin, branching trees with their delicate leaves and their small yellow flowers and the promise of the hard green sticks of fruit to come, she came down and leaned her hand on the narrow bark and stood still for a minute. The woman who lived in the ground-floor apartment came out of her kitchen and smiled at her. How many months now?

Tasneem turned slowly around. The woman was wringing out a wet piece of cloth and the wet skin of her hands glimmered in sun as she spoke.

Seven, said Tasneem. Two to go.

The woman looked up at her. Do you have family? Tasneem nodded without turning, thin morning light coming in through the forked limbs of the drumstick tree and sliding over her body. Sisters, mother?

Yes, said Tasneem.

The woman shook out the cloth and hung it on the stone ummi to dry. Are they treating you well? she asked, gesturing upward to the house.

Tasneem did not answer.

The old woman is hard to put up with, isn't she, said the woman. And the sons—ah, she shook her head as if they were something else now, they were terrible, and Tasneem said nothing, the fragile weight of the morning was beginning to settle on her, she could not speak.

The woman looked at her again and said, You wait here—I just made some tea, I'm going to get you some, and went inside.

There was a clattering down the stairs and Muhammad Ibrahim appeared in the doorway then like a vengeful god, his face thunderous. What are you doing down there? he shouted, leaving the house suddenly like that? Where is my breakfast and where is my shirt, you were supposed to iron my shirt!

Tasneem let go of the drumstick tree and turned, preparing to go.

The woman came hurrying out with her tea in an eversilver tumbler. You let her drink some tea now, she said. She's a pregnant lady—she needs some rest now and then.

She put the tea in Tasneem's hands. Drink it, go on, drink it.

Tasneem took a sip of it, it was so hot and the sweet steam of it singed her tongue and her husband lunged at her, reaching for her shoulder and delving instead into her hair, her thick long plait that hung to her waist, and pulled, and Tasneem's body jerked forward, the tea fell, shuddering and involuntary onto her arm, her elbow, and she screamed at the hard lick of heat that tore at her skin.

The woman had turned to stone, her mouth was open in shock and she leapt suddenly around and dragged the wet cloth off the ummi and took a hold of Tasneem's arm, the wet like a salve on the burn, smoothing it down. Tasneem started to cry. Ibrahim pushed the woman away and began to drag Tasneem into the stairwell and up the stairs, the woman beginning to scream at him. Let her go! My god, can't you see—throw water on her, she's burnt! Ibrahim swore at Tasneem for being so heavy he could barely lift her. She tried to shake him away. She tried to walk up the stairs on her own. But he was holding her, his fingers making deep ruts in her flesh. He would not let her go, her saree tripping both of them up the stairs, her body wrenched out of itself, out of the drumstick morning, and they went, stumbling, up the must-laden stairs, the wooden everlasting stairs into his world.

Later Tasneem remembered the painting that had hung on a wall of their house when they were little, framed in wood. Someone their father had met at his print shop, from another country, a foreigner, had visited the shop and given their father a painting. He'd told him he had painted it himself, that the trees in the painting grew outside his house.

The trees were like nothing they had ever seen, their trunks were straight and thin and tall, and the leaves scalloped and eaten at their edges like scoops of chlorophyll taken out by the painter. The sun came through the trees in amber resinous haze and made a clearing deep in the center. In the clearing was another painting. It blended invisibly into the first, green slopes shouldering into the haze of the green grape sun, and it led to an ocean, very blue, with sailboats in it. The slope of the hill above it was speckled with purple flowers in the grass. That was what you could see. You looked at the painting, at the thin dark trees and the golden sun and you saw the blue ocean, thundering and restless in the watery distance, and the little white sails of the boats, and the purple flowers in the grass.

When they were children they looked endlessly at that ocean, blue in the distance, and Tasneem believed it would be like this all their lives, you saw the trees first, hard and dark, and then you looked through them, and the sun came out and the clearing appeared, world blue with ocean. Blue was magic, she believed, because of the sky, soaked with color so delicate it ached sometimes, there, just between the bones of her heart, ribs stretched tight inside her, just to look at it. But then anything, said the voice inside her, anything was magic if you could look through it and see something else, whole in the distance.

She knew then, when the skin of her arm peeled and scabbed and filled with fluid, when the burn of that day's scald and destitution settled firmly in her flesh, a bruising, sprawling scar, she knew she hadn't reached the other side, she was still caught in the dark of the tree trunks, each small impossible flicker of sun making a silhouette of her limbs.

When she was young, she and her sisters had used to play in their holiday-time on the balcony of their second-floor apartment where their mother hung the clothes out to dry and the newspapers were stacked, destroyed by rain in old cardboard boxes falling apart near the piles of plastic cans and pickle bottles. Their mother collected these for the woman who bought cans and bottles for recycling for a few paise. They played with their bits of leaf and seed and yellow kadambaram flowers they picked from the neighbor's house in the back, or with the two raggedy dolls in the house, limbs dangling, clothes long-ago torn and hanging in threads, they made up stories of islands and strangers and being married and keeping house and being happy. This was alright, because their mother said nothing except at meal times when it was time to cook, or when the house needed cleaning, but their father didn't like to see the little girls playing outside, so they made sure they brought themselves in before he came home in the evening.

Later when Tasneem had begun already to feel the pressing

nuances of new shadows clustering, new swells and urns swirling inside her, she began to notice, slowly, how Saira and Shaheen still played outside, how they bathed in the evenings and
wore their tight churidhars and floating chunnis and sat outside
on the balcony, talking and posing and tossing their long hair, it
became something she joined in, shyly, not understanding, until
she saw the boys on the terrace across the way, and farther down,
the lone figure of a man, walking around on the rooftop, smoking, and it became suddenly exciting, a terrible thrill, just to stand
there. Their mother was suspicious, and found ways to draw them
in and keep them busy at something, but Tasneem, like Saira and
Shaheen, became clever and subtle and certain not to be caught
looking, she began to come out there in the evenings after school
when her mother was busy in the bedroom, folding clothes, or in
the kitchen, getting food ready for the boys.

Then it happened. She was alone, and this was the terrible irony
of it, because they had, the three of them, made a kind of uncon-
scious grouping of themselves on the balcony, as if in that wonder-
ful hollow of conversation created between the three of them they
were inventing each other and themselves, they were caught in
soft-focus light on a 70mm screen and the world sat in the dark,
watching, it was a ripple of power just being together, they were
wanderers, each of them the beautiful stranger in the movie, whose
face, glimpsed at a train window, etched itself in the hero's mind
like an exquisite, tragic mirage—and then, there she was, watering the plants on the balcony with a plastic mug of water from the
bathroom, six in the evening and the shape of her body burning
a curve into the coronal evening flare of sun, she wasn't aware of
the whistling until she turned, and saw them, three youths on the
street pointing up at her and whistling, crooning a Tamil love song,
and calling raucously out, Hey, sweet! What your name, baby? and
at the same time, a kind of thundering through the undergrowth
of the house—even before he raged out onto the balcony, sweating
and powerful, the true power after all, she knew it was her father.

He was furious. He believed she was doing this deliberately,
taunting, flirting with them, it was everything they lived in fear of,

cringed from the coincidence of, he unhooked the thick leather belt at his waist with the crude silver buckle and held her down with one hand, raining lashes down with the other, the other girls watching, horrified, his voice rising like a bitter hail of stones above them, cursing Tasneem, her mother, her sisters, the womb of vipers she had sprung from, the coiled serpent-evil in her leaping out now and forcing him to exert his power, when he had much better things to be doing, forcing him to keep his straying daughters in check when in fact he should let them, *just let them become prostitutes*, behaving as if there were no man in the house, no *father brother husband son* to keep them in check. The honor, he swore, the honor of his family, his long line of ancestors, going back to the sacred prophet and Allah himself, the honor had been unsullied until she came along, look at her now, she was threatening to be the ruin of them all, smearing his sacred name in the mud, her father's name, had she no respect for that? Her mother came into the room and threw herself at their father trying to wrench the belt from him, imploring him in the name of Allah to stop. He pushed her aside, panting, swearing, Tasneem fetal on the floor, a ball of bones and pain, the dragging-in of her sobs shaking the air. Then he stopped—suddenly, wiping his face, throwing the belt across the room, pushing past the girls and rushing outside. Saira looked at their mother, who said nothing at first. Then, going to Tasneem, she said, He was home early. I didn't know, how could I know, he was sitting downstairs with the old man Mr. Hanif from next door, something happened at work, he came home early.

Tasneem never went out onto the balcony after that, never again sun like fire on her skin and the beautiful unknown eyes of men on her, never again that glimpsing of the exquisite face from the distance, the power *the shoddy power that was no power* of being seen. Saira and Shaheen didn't either, not for a while, both parents watching them like vultures at the site of a death, and in a way it was a death, a death of soft-focus lighting and laughter, a death of attempt and desire, a death of expression, but later they found ways to return to that silken flaunting, when their father was at the mosque and their mother away at her sister's house. Tasneem stood at the window in the kitchen and looked out onto the street, the crowded rooftops, the cluster of houses, and through them and between them and apart from them always the rags and bones and spoonfuls of simmering blue sky, vivid with tribulation. In the iron window bars that kept the blue from her hands there was certainty and sleeping despair, a terrible coming to terms that Tasneem could feel coursing in the veins and doves of her breath when she thought of it.

Sometimes in the dark when the house was sleeping, she woke without knowing why and rose and went into the darkened kitchen with moonlight playing on the floor like a silver river, she opened the pot in the corner and scooped cold water into her tumbler. Then she walked, barefoot and careful to the window, and looked out over the silhouettes and the bare shiverings of trees and drank the cold water and looked up through the vertical bars in the window at the peeling stars. Her future felt like a vulture hovering, one hand over its darkened face, and the rampaging streets of the world approaching.

Still the sky was tearing apart now, and nothing could stop it. Her father's death screamed like a blue siren into the room, and the curtain at the door lifted.

She could hear the boy's footsteps, heavy and ominous, rising toward her. All around her there were piles of the blue paper, trunks, boxes, broken furniture, thick with dust. No one ever came into this room. But now it was hers, this was where she had begun to find sanctuary, waking without knowing why and coming up here to the loneliness. The pigeons roosted in the eaves just under the roof, and you could hear them from here, heavy flapping of their feathers and the soft cries they made. Sometimes they came and sat on the windowsill and she would sit quietly on the broken stool, the one with three legs pushed against the wall, and look at them. Always there was a handful of millet or wheat she put out on the windowsill.

The bird fluttered in her hands and all of a sudden she let it go. It flew around the room, rising and fluttering, and the *beat beat flicker* of its wings dazzled the broken air streaming in like fire from the window. The boy's steps on the stairs paused abruptly. *Who is there?* he called out. *Tasneem, Tasneem! Is that you up there?* Tasneem could see how the ribs and bones and anger of the poor street dogs, beaten past endurance, ascended slowly outside the window. Everywhere she looked, dreams were rising. She was no longer afraid. The bird flew excitedly around the room, and the shudder of breath he made fell smoothly around her. She walked without thinking toward the big blue porcelain vase that stood in the corner, an old vase that no one had wanted. She ran her fingers over the wide mouth of it and saw how there was room enough for the sky in there.

She knew that something had happened, something so minute and tender it had snapped the bearings of the world. Her father was dead. The blue sky had broken at last, it had come toward her. *I'm coming to find you, Tasneem* came the voice up the stairwell, and Tasneem stood still in the center of the room with the blue violence of sky bursting in all its power into the sanctuary and the air tearing in shreds into the room like paper, great lucent handfuls of blue paper, coarse and rough, tearing its brittle hands apart, and waited.

Pink Beads

AFTER SANDRA CISNEROS

ᛩ Look—pink beads, pastel and pearly pink, bright white bobbles in between, *two pink, one white*—look how we sit, threading our beads with fat chubby fingers, thin eight-year-old fingers, Prithika Shah and I, threading our Christmas bead chains for the school Christmas tree, eyes furious on tinsel pink and slick glossy white, pushing and pulling at fat beads, little beads, look how the sun comes through the bars in the window and lies in great yellow slabs on our skin.

We're going to be friends forever, I think, Prithika Shah whose mother brings a birthday cake to class and little green cups to drink lemonade in, a huge bean-shaped cake of chocolate that melts in your mouth, rich and dark, like chocolate does, and I who cannot speak because my mouth is thick with afternoons of reading and silence, brown dust and cloudings of it, vapors and smoke and blowing of it, flat on my tongue and grit in my eyes, we're going to be friends because she's come to sit beside me and her birthday dress is frilled and bowed and so very pink, sugar-candy pink at the throat, hibiscus-pink at the hem, there are flowery bouquets of scent in her nylon frills (a dab of her mother's perfume, amazing and adult), and I am wholly in her spell.

Such a pretty dress, I coo, and Prithika Shah tosses her velvety head with its two perfectly shiny braids on her pink shoulders and says, oh, do you mean this? I have two more you know, from Bombay, that are prettier!

Prettier than this? I say, and Prithika Shah says *one has bright orange sequins and the other has lace*, and I sit thinking of the mystery of it, rooms full of color and acres of lace, and if I knew a word for a tone there in fourth standard in Our Lady of Fatima Convent in Secunderabad in 1972, I would say *smug*, or *her voice was fat with complacence*, but I don't, I say *omigosh* in the purest of awe.

Pink sugar dress with frills.

Lunch that her driver brings *hot hot hot* to our open lunchroom where the trees bend right across and the crows come hungry and cawing.

And after History comes her mother, who looks nothing like mine (gray-haired, working-woman, prematurely gray, school-teacher who wears the same weekday sarees over and over), her young mother, slim and cool in her fresh turquoise saree and vivid flower earrings. I want to go home with Prithika's mother! I want to visit again that cool yellow tiled kitchen of hers where the counters stretch in an immaculate square all round the room and we sit at a smooth marble-topped table and sip ice-clinking orange Fantas with red-and-white-striped plastic straws. Two months since I met Prithika, and I've already been to the beautiful house with the lotus pond in the center of the driveway and the dazzling magenta bougainvillea massed in the garden and the white stone swan in the water and the mali snipping a big red rose each for Prithika and me, water like silver droplets on the petals and the deep rose-scent of it so piercingly sweet you want to bathe in it, sleep in it, right there in the sun, eat that brilliance of red.

I tell my mother about Prithika's house and I don't think she understands, her mouth goes quiet and her eyes *flash flash flash* so I won't say anymore, I keep it inside of me, big still spaces with the light from the French doors coming in yellow and thick as honey into the room, onto the white eyelet lace on the bedspread and the big stuffed rabbit on the pillow, small secret places like the velvety pink inside the big conch shell on the window, with its mouth of open marble and the ocean in its mouth washing up against your ear. Far from our house with the cramped rooms that ring with clatter and din, full with the overflowing shelves and the tall wooden cupboard in the corner of the room and the three beds in a row against the shuttered window, and the flecked black and white mosaic of our tiles worn to shadow and gray by our feet, over and over, busy anonymous cream.

Nobody understands why anymore.

Why I want to stay over at Prithika's house, or want a bean-shaped chocolate cake for my birthday or a pink frilly dress. Not even myself, not anymore, I just know I want them, I couldn't spell out why if I tried. Nobody knows what I want because I tell no one, the words sleep in my mouth like sleepy winged things, translucent and fluttering, silver and dust on their edge. No one asks, no one listens, and I hold my want tight inside me like a white handkerchief pressed clean, raw still tangle of want grating like breath in my lungs.

Maybe no one asks because there's no one at home in the afternoons when I let myself in and read in the silence, listening to the steps of the two-year-old children in the flat overhead. I know it's time for my parents to come home bringing my twin sisters from kindergarten with them when the light curls into itself in the sky and dusk eats the words by the window. All too soon it's time for homework, time for dinner, time for sleep.

All of a sudden it feels a bit shameful to be living in a flat on the fourth floor of a building with no whisper of a driveway in sight or a pond with purple lotuses or a kitchen with marble counters. It's not a place I can bring Prithika to. The whole idea makes my stomach shrink inside, like a balloon's skin when the air comes rasping and wheezing out and it sinks and shivers into its crumpled self at the end, no air in it, imagine how the walls would crowd in on her, pale and useless in their regular off-white, so close and sinister, how the dark, nail-scarred furniture in the living-room would choke and crush her, how the ridiculous curtains with their frayed edges and pathetic little cameos of people in rice fields would smother her, how my two younger sisters, whispering and staring and incapable of common courtesy would shock her. Oh dreadful thought!

Then something happens and I begin to help Prithika Shah with her homework. One day her report at school says Failed in Mathematics, Failed in Science, Failed in English. Sister Maria from New Delhi who is tall and thin talks to her mother in Hindi in the middle of the day. Her mother looks once, hopefully, across at me, as I sit beside Prithika and stare at how her long satin braid shines against her slippery pink nylon saree. The next thing I know we have begun to do our homework together at lunch break and for an hour after school in the afternoons because her mother asks my mother the next day at school and my mother agrees. It'll help you, my mother says, as if it wouldn't help *her*, and her mother beams. We are having so many functions, this and that, so many relatives, weddings and all, she cannot do homework by herself, and my mother frowns and says, There's nothing wrong with doing the homework in the lunch break. There's nothing wrong with Lizbeth helping.

It's funny but Prithika seems to understand everything so much better when I explain to her. I spend a lot of time explaining triangle theorems and photosynthesis and why water condenses on the outside of a cold-water glass and Prithika listens. For me it's a game we play. For her it's a way to get her homework done. Her driver brings tea for us in a silver flask and hot samosas in the afternoons, I feel singled out as the other girls leave, looking at us, and we sit in the lunchroom with our books. I begin to feel as if this is the way it was meant to be, I'm special because I can teach, it almost makes me feel it's okay not having a pink sugar dress from Bombay with frills or a house with red roses and a lotus pond in front of it.

My fingers slip, the beads spurt and spill right across the painted yellow table and onto the shiny red linoleum floor, little blobs of pink and silver lapping along, jostling and pushing, running downslope across the classroom like rivulets of water. Prithika and I are down on our hands and knees, we are laughing hysterically and we are running up against beads with the flat of our palms and our square, little-girl knees, we are chasing pink shiny beads running away from us.

It is only seven years to the day when Prithika Shah will go away to her grandmother's village to be married at fifteen going on sixteen in a red and gold brocade saree drawn across her mehendi'd face and heavy ropes of gold around her neck. Her six children and her mother-in-law and her several relatives who will live with her and her businessman husband who is fifteen years older than her wait just around the corner of her life in her ordained, implacable future, in a place where there are no more French windows, no yellow sun on eyelet lace, where the women cover their heads when they talk.

So who is to say what happens when our fingers slip, when the beads we held so carefully in our hands shudder and spill away from us? I never knew that one day my lonely afternoons of silence would add up to words, step upon step of stories and words, that I would turn into a reporter one day, of other people's stories and fictions of my own, find from the ruins and desolations of silence something writhing in my blood for language, a whole lexicon of breaths, all of the cluttered rooms I have lived in to seep like ink, a finger bleeding, into my canvas. That I would grow up to name Prithika's life privileged, orthodox, surrendering, and mine working-class, struggling, questioning. I never saw how our lives would move so sharply away from each other we would never stay friends.

But it is afternoon, the sun is yellow and burning on the wooden desks, on our pinafored shoulders, and Prithika Shah and I are oblivious, we are chasing pink beads, little white beads across the floor not knowing they are worlds at our eight-year-old fingertips, evanescent and restless, rushing away, shiny and slick, with mighty wills of their own, far, far, away from us.

Esther

༄ It happens after midnight, like it has so many times before, on this night when my mother's away in the hospital at her father's dying bedside, and we're alone in the Madras house, my sister and I, with Kanthi, my grandfather's old servant-lady, who sleeps in the hall, two rooms away, on the floor.

Click. Scrape. Click.

Then sharper, more convincingly, as before: *Click Clack. Click Clack.* We hear the footsteps of death on the terrace, they are cool and hard, sound of heeled sandals on brick, the sound of resolution.

I wake and look across at my sister, huddled under her sheet. Moonlight streams down my face, shivers on Krista's form, plays in a silvery tangle of light and shadow on the wall. The window is open. Through bars I see the high three-quarter moon, swept-away shreds of cirrus and bright sky around it. Leaves of the cotton trees sway. There's a wind outside, rustling through sheets, breathing a cool touch on our skin.

Upstairs the dogs cry, a pained, whimpering sound. Zorro and Slim, our rescued mongrels, who like to sleep on the terrace and hear her each time, just as we do, as clearly as if she had just left the room. *Click Clack. Click Clack.*

It is 1978. I am almost fourteen, my sister is eight. We have come down from Bangalore to my grandfather Roderick's house in Madras a little earlier this summer than usual because he is sick, he is dying, and my mother is his only child and wants to be here with him.

Her footsteps click on the terrace sharp as gunshot, definite as the play of light going up at windows—*one-two one-two* as the lady of the house climbs upward.

But Esther is not the lady of the house, not anymore. Esther is not alive. Esther, my grandfather's long-dead wife, my mother's mother, was not even someone we knew.

My mother speaks of her often, and knows we can hear her now, walking about at night. We are not alone in this. She has often told us about what she loosely terms her "visions." Not dreams, she'd correct, these are real faces she saw, real people she heard. Not dream-figures. She'd wake from a dream sometimes, and her dream would open to an afterlife thick with long-departed relatives, climbing over the windowsill, standing beside her bed, curled up in 2 a.m. armchairs in the sleeping parlor. Once she saw old Mrs. Zulfikhar next door who died at eighty-three in her sleep (*wearing a bright blue saree—seventeen, maybe eighteen, but it was her, she was smiling, I saw her face*), she saw her grandfather for years (*leaning on his cane, wearing the white suit he wore everyday to his work during British times in the Post Office*), she saw my uncle Terence Ratnam who died prematurely of a heart attack at forty-five (*sitting in the armchair, sipping tea at our house, reading the newspaper*).

We are like her, she says. We hear without knowing we can. Because we are children. To us the stars are white stones still, half-raised, half-buried in the sky's dark. Our hands, unsoiled with the knowledge of the world, have not learned to press firm on our eyes, ears, minds yet. But mostly, she says, we hear the ghost of Esther Kanamma Samuel walk the dark corridors of the after-dead in this house where she was born because we are *her* children, we have inherited her skin.

All our lives our mother has half-believed she is psychic and half-believed she dreams. It is no clear thing, this feeling, and now she's gifted it to us, an amorphous certainty of stepping across borders and limits of the mummified heart, not too certain of what we're seeing.

It is like the feeling I had when I opened the old falling-apart crate on the terrace one afternoon last week. It had probably been thrown out by my irate grandfather, sifting through his things and deciding he didn't need to keep this. The wood was damp with rain, planks falling, nails pulled apart. Inside I saw sheets of old notebook paper, tied up in string. I saw sprawling words on yellowing paper, the fine blue ink of another time spoiled and rotting at edges.

My mother told me they were Esther's long-ago letters to herself. She took the sopping-wet packet away from us, put the ceiling fan on in the dining-room and dried the pages. She shooed us from the room, smoothed the crinkly sheets, squinted through dissolving ink, cried when she read the words—through the white cheese-crepe curtain I saw her.

I don't know the true story of Esther, I never will, although I grow up to read the scraps of her letters, sift through her photographs, hear everything about her my mother knows to tell. Krista and I have never heard Esther's footsteps before either, although we've spent many summers here. But the whole of the past few weeks, since we arrived, we've woken at night to the sound of a woman's footsteps across the terrace and the dogs making strange sounds, whimpering, questioning, shout-barking.

So perhaps my mother is right. Perhaps we've graduated now in some way and never knew it. Perhaps we'll be privy now to whisperings, barely-breathed, the afterthoughts, teeming undertones of the universe. Like her, to live on a border between worlds, hear the comings and goings of souls long-stilled. Summon them at will perhaps, have them open at our touch like hands parting, a flurry of birds, wings rising and rising.

I am not soothed by this feeling. I shiver as I lie and watch the silvery moon climb the waking, stretching mound of Krista-shadow underneath her sheet.

Tonight is the night my grandfather dies. I do not know this, not yet. What I do know is I have spent this summer dreaming of my grandmother Esther, as I hear her story, finally, in bits and pieces, at night, from my mother. What I know is the moon is nearly full tonight and slides easy as milk over our skin. We wake to this light, and for once it feels like the whole truth about Esther comes toward us.

Esther is nineteen in the picture, taken three months after her marriage, that hangs, framed in teak, in the hall. Her mouth held straight, wavy hair pulled back in studied crests and knotted at the nape. Her eyes quiet, irises gray, like my mother's.

Her eyes look directly at me, clear and still. I walk to the far left where the radio sits, to the crowded right where the sofa crouches, low and green—she cannot lift her eyes from mine, we are glued, as if by ether, a mesmeric substance sticky with compulsion. I sift through photographs for expressions in her eyes. Here she is, leaning against the front door, saree flying, looking into the sky. *Such soft dreaming eyes.* Here, with a child on her shoulder, sitting on the front-steps. *Mildly quiescent eyes.*

Here, alone, leaning against the parapet wall on the terrace. Her face calm. *Quiet, remembering eyes.* Once, with a group of other women, my mother's aunts and cousins, at a wedding, all laughing, her eyes opening up the calm pool of her face, surprised in a smile: *briefly flying eyes.*

She wasted away, my mother says. She shriveled up inside, she died of grief.

These were the kinds of things my mother told me for years, about Esther.

A hard thing to believe, when you're eight or nine. Such shimmering in that smile. Could a woman, grown, evaporate on whim?

What was grief, to swallow a body whole, erase such complexities of light?

She fell ill, my mother would, slightly, elaborate. She kept falling ill, it was one thing after another, the flu, jaundice, malaria, grief blew out her body's flame, stamped it out.

Falling ill all the time was her grief, then? For years, my mother wouldn't elaborate.

Each time we came to visit my grandfather, each summer we spent in the house, I looked up at night into the gray desolation of her eyes. What hue of grief elicited ends like this, spelled out death in limbs?

As if to keep the mystery alive, my mother would hint at even more tragic ends. *It is only the unfinished who return,* she would say. *She did not finish her life.*

All I had of my posthumous Paatiamma Esther then for years were those eyes, beautiful, troubled eyes, looking out from her portrait into the room. I often stood in the hall by myself and looked up at her, searched the room to see what assembled in her gaze. The long sofa, medium sofa, cabinet with silver trophies and medals, photographs. The old red rocking-chair on the veranda.

Forever she looks, I'd think. That long haunting of her look does not expend itself in mine. It ricochets still, off these walls, this room: she's really not transfixed in time. Yes, unlike the many dead clustering behind her in the black velvet albums of my mother's childhood, here in our hall portrait, Esther seemed to be merely the golden radioactive death of rock under the earth's shifting crust. Down deep, molten, I think, *she's still alive.* Her saree pours its silky watermelon-pink, hot-tongue pink, inside-tomato-pink brightly down from her waist. She stands still, she smiles. Day after day, like a mirror's still return, pungent shadow without name. Present and not-present. When I look into her eyes at night I can almost believe she's right there in the room with us.

But hearing Esther's high-heeled sandals mark time on the terrace has not been the only change this year. So many things have been different. My mother's sudden over-protectiveness for one.

Ever since we came to the house, she's been increasingly watchful and worrisome, guarding over Krista and me as if we might fall to pieces and break if she lifted her eyes from us.

A *little* light, she says to us in private, not turned black in the sun. I want my girls' skins to stay light, not dark. Across the garden's space, she calls: Krista, Leeza, better come in out of the sun! For minutes she hovers by the back door, watching us, Zorro and Slim drooping their tails behind her, languid from the heat.

Even this, that I chafe against, over-protecting of our female skin, is a ruse, I've learned. At four in the afternoon, she's back early from the private hospital where she spent all day, tending her father, hair still coiled into its business knot. I sigh. Every summer in Madras we play at Reena and Laila's house, but now everything has changed.

She walks up to the line of shrubbery between their house and ours, frowns some more when she sees Sumit hovering over my shoulder as I scratch pandi squares into loose earth with a twig, she calls across the garden's flowering space to us.

Sumit is watching a copious trail of red ants as I turn. He steals the twig from my hands, blurs the line I've drawn to exclude their frantic spill from our pandi-jumping squares (in a dim effort to save them from our feet). When she calls from the red-rose bush, I turn, dismayed, I see her eyes, a few yards away, on us.

I know what this means, what panicky flight her thoughts are on, strumming like a crazed dragonfly an inch from my skin. Sumit is Reena's cousin, he is down from Calcutta for the summer. Everything has changed, I think, since he came.

Who is that boy, she said, the first time she saw him in Reena's garden. Frowning, turning from the window to look sharply at us. It was the day she started to make brassieres for me (my mother never said *bra* to us, not even when we were all grown up and bought our own underwear from Fountain Plaza and Spencer's), sitting at the sewing machine by the window, slicing cloth into triangular shreds. I knew I wouldn't want to wear these contraptions as I saw one take shape under her hands, wide cotton band with unnatural cones on it, I went up to the window to look. Sumit was in a red checked shirt, lying on his back in the grass, squinting earnestly up at a squirrel in Reena and Laila's guava tree. She pursed her lips as I looked, stopped the busy hum of her pedal, pulled me away, hand on my elbow. Go read your library books, she said, you have to return them soon.

She wouldn't say the word *boy* again that day, but every now and then, I could see her thinking it. I'd never really been friends with a boy before, and my mother was proud of it. Boys around her girls made her uncomfortable. These days boys around me while I was around her had started to make me uncomfortable too. I could see already what she was thinking, tell she thought there were dangers here, she was trying to protect me from them.

If she could have her way, I knew, she'd lock us inside the house each time she went to the hospital. She had said as much to us. But Reena's mother wanted us. She made ginger biscuits for us, flecked with lemon peel, and fresh muruku, straight off the stove, she served us grape crush in tiny crystal glasses. She scolded, cajoled: I need some company for my children! She was older than my mother, and larger. Both these, especially the radial spread of her bulk, I think, contrived to root, substantiate her in ways my mother, ambivalent, anxious, thin as a reed, felt she couldn't resist each time we were invited.

So part of the day stayed ours, while my grandfather was ill. When my mother returned, usually at five or six, she looked for us.

There are roses growing on the bush beside us, sultry burst of flame as I turn, hooked thorns on a stem, I smell the red sweetness of their scent. I want you to come inside This Minute, my mother says, you'll get a headache playing in the sun!

The sun is soft, a watery dream on my skin, I'm half-asleep in its swell.

Elizabeth, Kristine! In-Side Now!

Your *Moth*er's calling, Reena says. You better go!

I shuffle reluctantly to my feet. Sumit is saving red ants with his stick. My sister is tearing a shoeflower apart, its yellow pollen vying with dust on her hands, red tongues lolling in shreds on her wrist. I sigh, petals drop about us, I lift her to her feet.

Sunday morning after church, my mother tells me they fell in love. It's true! Of course they never met. Of course it was an arranged marriage. It was 1934, *ma,* what do you expect?

We are sitting in the hall after lunch. She has her sewing machine pulled up to her chair and is stitching a saree blouse, I am reading a book and staring idly up at Esther.

Both? I ask. They both fell in love?

She's quiet for a moment, foot-pedal still, hand adjusting blouse under the needle, up and down. Esther loved Roderick, she says finally, as if reciting an ancient fairy-tale, intoning the names of her mother and father. Who knows how it happened? Who knows when? She was attached to him. He was her life.

And he?

She sighs, clamps her needle down, starts to run the treadle with her feet. He didn't want to get married for a long time. He was too busy with his law books. But she was very beautiful, and he must have looked at her and seen that. Right from the start, from that moment in church, when they saw each other.

I didn't say anything, just watched the saffron-yellow cotton fly under her hands as she fed it, feet pumping, to the needle. How else could they have made a child, she says, above the flying hum.

She means, by *the child,* herself. I have heard about their wedding, how perfect it was. I look at the calm Grecian folds of the ivory curtain in the studio where Esther stands, ivory pillar on which her hand rests. In her eyes I imagine the faint hint of a smile, hear bells ring in the distance, church bells. Rain, very light, clouds like gloves rubbing their fingers together and letting a drizzle of moisture slip through.

She is wet stepping out of the car, lifting her cream and gold tissue-silk saree high above wet gravel at the entrance to the church. She walks up the aisle with drops of water in her veil. There are people everywhere: eyes, jewelry, light from the chandeliers tossed among oceans of silk. When she looks through the veil at the people, flowers, marble angels and plaques, she sees a thousand points of light, blurry and wet, winking at her. She sees Roderick, whom she's never seen before.

Wound to a spiral of quiet until this moment, her curiosity untwists, probes intensely through the veil for a sense of him. He is thin, occluded. Yellow rosebud in his lapel, shirt incandescent. She feels, instantly, the deep, unmoving silence of him. It draws her as she looks, invokes in her an obscure sense of alliance. She senses, inventing, that he too, against his will, is *brought* by his parents to this moment: oldest son, alone until thirty-one, delivered abruptly from insularity to marriage. She looks at his face, tremulous, intellectual, the moment is transcendent.

It is this moment then that seals her future, ties her inescapably to the need of him, not the vows, thali, ring: desire rises in her like a summons. He turns his head slightly, meets her eyes, gaze coursing the silken length of her. Veiled interest in his eyes blinding. The church fades around her in that moment, she feels the heat of his body through the tissue of her saree, veil, she draws in her breath. The organ's hum decreases, the pastor begins to speak.

It takes the insistent scent of jasmine rising from her own neck to recall her. The Reverend Edward Jones, who speaks to his congregation every Sunday without fail of his native Wales, is reading their vows to them. Esther looks down, past his knobby pink hands on the prayer book to the masculine edge of Roderick's hairy wrist poking through white cuffs. Heat from the bright lights of the chandeliers begins to speak to her. She feels it gather in clumps and handfuls, at her armpits, diaphragm, thighs. When she whispers *I do* to Roderick, she is emitting a quiet steam, a cloud of vapor that sizzles out of her damp and heated clothes and hangs in shivery brilliance about her body.

She is the cloud, I tell myself. She is the wisp of faintly mauve on the mango tree, lilted, swung in space, barely grounded. It is two nights later, one night after Laila's birthday party on Monday. We are on the terrace. Waking to footsteps, clutching each other's hands, we slid open the latch to the courtyard door, slipped into starlight. We followed her upstairs in the dark, hand to mouths, hearts loud in our chests, dogs in front of us. We would not have done this if the dogs hadn't been sleeping in our room and woken us. They roused when she started to *click-clack* across the terrace. Slim came and licked my face. Zorro ran excitedly round the room, yipping and whining. They led the way outside. Zorro, brown and white, a fluffy terrier, kept his tail down but crept bravely in front. Slim, taller, and more of a mix with straight-up ears and a sleek physique, had his ears back and walked with careful steps behind.

We couldn't see her. But we heard her heels *click click* on the terrace floor and pause, before the mango tree. We saw the leaves sway in the sudden breeze, saw the cloud break loose from the field of clouds high in the star-pearled sky and settle like mist on mango leaves.

The dogs broke away from us, ranged themselves under the mango tree, barking.

She never became a shape I could recognize, never looked at us. I couldn't say I had seen eyes, hands, a body poised in warning.

But I felt strangely that we had seen the cloud of her, the breathing.

We stood, a few yards from the mango tree, looking. The dogs barked and barked. Neither of us stopped them. (The dogs barked like this every night anyway. My mother, I was sure, was too used to it to investigate.) There was no moon that night and except for here-and-there clouds the sky was dark.

Leeza, this is scary, Krista says, let's go to bed.

You go, I say, I'll be down in a second.

By myself? Krista asks, doubtfully.

Take the dogs!

The dogs go down with her but come running up again after she goes inside. I linger on the terrace then, dogs lying down beside me, I look through the slats in the parapet wall where the party was yesterday. Where Reena and Laila's garden is. A smudge of green, an openness.

It was Laila's seventh birthday. The guava tree had been strung with lights, the rose bush decked in crepe. Reena's father had brought his stereo out to the garden and guarded it, smiling fixedly when we approached to watch the LPs spin, black circles wobbling. He stood by the table with the cake on it, bright rainbow party plates, pile of balloons that needed to be blown, open ice box with crystal chunks in it. He offered me limeade twice when Sumit and I, sweating from our game, came up to the table, shooing us away from the cake. *Lucee in the Skai with DY-Monds*, screamed the speakers on the table.

The cake was pista-green, there was a full layer of crushed nuts on it, just above the cream, I tasted the tangy sweetness of my drink and looked greedily at it through my frosted glass.

No, no, said Reena's mother, when my mother made dissenting noises, they must all play together, there's no fun otherwise! She meant, the girls with the boys, of course. My mother's social face came on, a tightly neutral mask with a Colgate smile etched on it. She sat beside Reena's mother, refraining from excessive speech, twisting her lace handkerchief in her hands.

It was a family party, there were many children. The ladies in their bright billowy nylon sarees sat on white wicker chairs at the edge of the lawn, sipping their Fantas and lime juice with us. The men stole inside to mix more potent drinks.

I hid by the rosebush with Reena and Sumit, we saw clearly we were older, more decorous than the rest of the kids, screaming, running around, we'd never been so indiscreet at their age, had we, we were talking about the universe (but where did it all come from!) which led to God and immediate mayhem (and what was Behind God? And What God are you talking about, precisely? Does it matter which God? Whether it's Allah or God God or Shiva or Vishnu or whoever? Isn't God all the same? Leeza, how come your God alone is God God?) which led Aunty to ferret us out, Come on, children! They're playing Chain, go play with everyone!

Was I a child? I felt very grown-up these days, almost fourteen, almost in tenth standard. I ran with the rest of them, zigzagging, evading capture, but I was finally caught, Sumit's hand clutching mine, surprisingly strong, holding me in the Chain as we flew across grass, pulled in opposing directions by the erratic wills of those at either end, dragged and bumped along. Conscious of the lights as I flew, heat we dove through, drum of music in the air, still pool of my mother's eyes. Once I saw my mother's face, frozen, orange drink and white hanky clutched together in one hand, frowning. I thought mostly it was because of her I was ultra-conscious of the proximity of our bodies, Sumit's and mine, fiery palms and fingertips where our hands touched. But soon I stopped thinking about her. Lights spun redly in my head as I ran, space whirled and pulsed, I felt as if a string of stars crackled and shone along the line from Sumit's hand upward to his heart. I looked up at him, licks of hair wet on his skin, spectacles pushed down his nose, cheekbones gleaming, our eyes met, bright, alive, we smiled. The whole mysterious universe spiraled down to the tensile contact between us, slide of sweat between our palms, salt sweetness of it.

My mother must have been watching us, for soon after the cake, sweet pista cream of it, she came up and said in a steely held-in way, go find your sister, Leeza, we have to go. And so we did, despite Reena's mother's protests. I didn't say anything to Sumit as I left, nor did he. I glanced back at him once. He was at the cake-table, wolfing cake with Reena, whose father seemed to have abandoned it once it was cut.

From the terrace I peer at the garden, empty now. The square wooden table is still sitting outside, devoid of its contents. There's a scrap of white at its foot where a twist of crepe paper gleams. The string of lights, shut off, trails blindly across the guava tree. I can't help but think of my mother, sitting there with her drink, frowning at us. Coming over to get me away from the dangerous scourge of boys. I wonder if *her* mother ever did that to *her*. Then I remember. My mother was brought up by her grandmother and father in a silent house. Her mother was Esther. When my mother was nearly fourteen, the age I am now, her mother died. When she was twenty-three, she was married away like her mother to a man she'd never known too well. She had met him in church a few times before the engagement. He had just finished his residency and got a job as a psychiatrist in Bangalore. He saw her in church with her grandmother and asked for her hand. It was all very genteel. Her father said yes. She served him tea and sweet orange soji with fried raisins and cashewnuts one afternoon, talked to him in church. Then she put her veil on, slid a ring on his hand, settled down with him. She left her house in Madras, moved to Bangalore. And what of my father? His family was full of doctors, teachers, college professors, researchers, lawyers. But like him they had all got into arranged marriages. Even my older cousins, I knew, on my father's side, had mostly got married that way.

Now it seemed my mother wanted to raise us, her daughters, toward that very ideal: the arranged marriage, bland in its certainties, boundaried and known, calmly controlled. To whom Sumit, *a boy a boy a boy,* is a dangerous flicker of the unknown. Kinetic, unpredictable, rogue streak of current dancing erratically into the still rooms of her daughters' lives. Liable to wreak havoc, set walls on fire, *alter* us.

From the mango tree, shadows loom. Does my mother really believe we're going to fall in with arranged marriages, I wonder. At school, when my friends talked of boys, weddings, futures, I was the first to laugh it all off and walk away. Letting your parents find a boy for you—what a thought! It sounded silly. But then the whole topic of marriage sounded silly. Too far away. I shrugged it off easily while my friends sat around at lunch and talked about weddings for ages, I went to the library instead.

My thoughts move sharply from arranged marriages to Sumit. The memory of Sumit's hand in mine races along the edge of my mind, hot stream of lightning. At the party he made the whole night come alive.

Krista comes to the bottom of the steps and shouts in a whispery kind of way, Leeza, you better Come Inside Now, I'm going to lock the door.

I move, dogs tumbling to the steps ahead of me, I look one last time at the garden below. The white twist of crepe attached to the table-leg flutters vertically like a snake. Starlight plays faintly on the grass.

The next night my mother pours tamarind sauce over the mound of hot white rice on my plate, picking out garlic buds for me with her spoon. I smoosh fried chili potatoes with my fingers and eat. They were just like any other couple, she says. This was the house they came to, after their marriage. They lived here throughout, in this house. They had a child. It was normal.

She died of grief, I say. How could it be normal?

My mother shakes her head. She is preoccupied. She has come home late, she put together a quick puli sauce and potatoes, she wants to make sure we have fresh food for every meal, but she's tired from her long day in the nursing-home. She looks as if her mind is still there, or somewhere else. She talks more and more about her mother without my prompting her to. As if it were her mother, not father, who is dying.

She pushes her straying hair behind her ear and I look at her tired eyes and realize there was a life she lived, right here in this house, with her mother and father, when Esther was alive, that I know nothing about. That is coming back to her now.

That night after dinner I wander back into the hall and look up at Esther. The soft teal blue of the studio background looks a bit like an ocean behind her. On top of it she bobs, with her ivory column and curtains, pink saree pleated, hair calmly waved, her eyes secret and still. I try to imagine her living here in this house with my grandfather, a younger version of him, and I'm stumped. I have known my grandfather only as a remote, lonely figure used more to his books and newspapers than his family. Who sat at tables at mealtimes and said no word sometimes, grunted when questioned, lost his temper too easily with his mother or daughter if they crossed him, shooed me and Krista and our cousins away when we came too near or tried to converse with him.

Whose house nevertheless brims richly over with Esther, the grandmother we never knew, as if in some vague attempt to still her unquiet spirit. (*Her silks in the almirah. Her paintings on the wall. Her portrait in the hall. Her pictures in the album.*) Yet I cannot imagine him speaking with warmth or being in love with Esther. He was always closed, eyes remote, when people spoke to him. I feel it must have been a little different than my mother is telling me.

It is not till years later when I am twenty-seven and married to a man I choose myself that I hear what my mother does not tell me then, at fourteen, that I make up for myself.

Esther lived with Roderick. Slept with him, woke with him. She could not say she knew him. The tangle of limbs that preceded sleep was hers, ritual surrender to want behind the closed door of their room. Steady speech of skin upon skin. From the start, these were the ways she learned who Roderick was, by the clutch of his hand on her spine, languor in his eyes, words on her shoulder when he slept. The room gave him to her, single room that was theirs in the Samuel household that housed all the brothers and their wives: the room, the night, the bed.

But it was brief, a fenced-in gift. Day's brilliance stole him without a qualm, removed him from her reach. It was as if they had a secret life together in the night and everything changed in the morning. He just never spoke to her. It was how he was brought up by his family. He was brought up to be a man, to keep his thoughts to himself. He expected this. Not to be questioned, or be asked to speak if he didn't feel like it. When she met his eyes in daylight they were closed, iron gates shut tight against her probing.

I sit on the sofa, staring at Esther. My mother comes into the hall and sits beside me. The clock begins to chime the hour. Eleven chimes. She looks at Esther and sighs. He never told her about Suraiya, she says, softly, as if speaking to herself. She found out by herself.

Who was Suraiya? I don't really expect an answer. My mother is used to cutting off conversations with her children. Right now I'm not used to her confiding in me. I watch her fold the newspaper that lies spread out on the coffee table in front of us.

She was a street-woman, she says, she sold guavas on the street. He became friends with her.

I frown. How?

Everyone knew Suraiya, my mother says. She was a pretty woman, and if someone with a cart in the marketplace is good-looking, they stand out. Everyone on the street knew her. I heard about her from your great-grandmother. She was fair, like a North Indian. Kashmiri, they called her. I suppose he could not help noticing her. My mother looks up at Esther. And everyone must have noticed him too, paying attention to her.

The first time he bought guavas from her, he attempted flattery: Did you know you look like the actress Nargis? She looked away from him, did not smile.

He'd often seen her tend her husband's cart at noon, saree pulled tight across her shoulders, beautiful face impassive. He wanted to look into her eyes. These guavas, he said, you grow them yourself?

No, she said, my husband buys them from the main market in Broadway.

And where do they come from, he asked.

She would not encourage his clumsy advances. She would not raise her head. From Kodaikanal, she said, from the hills. Her hands moved swiftly, weighing, wrapping fruit in newspaper, cutting twine from a spool. Colored glass bangles glittered on her wrist, silver rings on her fingers. Her nails were freshly painted red, Roderick stared at them.

He stopped often at the cart after that, both when she was alone and with customers. His courtship was flagrant, effusive. Everyone knew about it. But Suraiya was a woman used to male attention, to deflecting it. This resistance, of course, proved her undoing. Unlike Esther, whom he thought of as transparent, steadily available, Suraiya was closed, a distant kingdom. He started to dream about taking her to the movies.

Slowly, he began to spend more and more time with her. My mother would stay up all night waiting for him.

Didn't she know, about the guava-lady?

Everyone knew, my mother says. Even his mother, the servants. But they kept it from her.

That first evening Roderick was late, Esther sat on the front step, waiting for him. The sky was dark, all the rooms in the house lit. Roderick's mother approached, asked her to eat. It was nine then, the mood at the table quiet. No one spoke. She returned to her vigil. The street gave up its sound of passing feet, for an hour, maybe two. The white glare of the street lamp outlined the wall. It was past eleven when the gate creaked and swung open. Roderick's light step on the path stalled when he saw her.

What happened, she said, where have you been? I didn't think you would be so late!

The house was asleep now, behind her.

Roderick took her arm and led her indoors, to their room. There's no need for you to worry, he said. You should have gone to bed.

But where have you been?

He sat on the side of the bed, paused in the act of pulling off his shoes, one blue sock in hand. He looked at her, his daytime face unfolding. The clock in the hall chimed the half hour. A trickle of sand fell out of the sock.

Tell me!

His face stretched tautly over rage, a refusal of her questions. She saw what hovered in his intention then, and instantly, inwardly retreated. She imagined him raising his voice, then his hands to her, shattering the silence of the night, waking the house. She had seen him convulsed with rage before, with his mother, younger brothers, the servant-girl. His mother, cowed, would retreat, muttering about being a Christian woman, about *keeping the peace*. She would take Esther's arm, look earnestly into her eyes, it is up to you, she would say, you must not provoke him.

A small pool of sand was collecting beneath his feet. Beach sand, she thought, mesmerized, not knowing what else to think.

He did not speak, but pulled the other sock off, stuffed each in its shoe. She stood by the open window. A curl of wind touched her shoulder, lifted the voile of her saree. From somewhere down the street, she heard the faint rise of a flute. Nothing from Roderick. Blank eyes, calm resumption of the night's ablutions. He went to the bathroom, she heard the water running. He came back into the room, wiping his face with a towel, looked at her with those blank eyes of his, saying nothing.

Then she knew this in itself was speech, a kind of defiance. She felt it like the stem of a woody plant in her hands, growing in the desert. She felt its wiriness and muscle, its ugly growing. She lay down, hands under her head, facing the window. She could see how it stemmed from the torrential admonitions of his parents to always do what they wanted. She could tell it was a weed he'd tended long in their garden, a hardy, resilient weed, purple at the throat and bitter with blood, it was heavy, unsprouting, this silence. It was a way of being. Not an excuse, but powerful, a form of action.

Roderick switched off the light and lay beside her. He did not touch her. She froze, all the strength and questions in her receding. She had no tools, she thought, to combat his silence with. But her own. And of what use was it?

It was the night of the new moon, a darkness. The palms outside the window tossed slightly, expunging stars.

The next evening we sit in the front garden just before the sun sets, air transfused with a golden light, low, soft, heatless. My mother says, Esther planted these, pointing her watering can at the balsam and crotons, as she washes the day's dust from the brightly-colored leaves. Zorro and Slim lie in the grass at her feet. Krista and I sit on the front steps, stringing jasmine buds on thread, watching her idly. She has come home a little earlier than yesterday from the hospital. In the sun's intimate light she looks both exhausted and ethereal. Sun glows on her hair and face.

My father is fading, she says.

Did he talk to you today? We have visited my grandfather in the nursing-home once, the day after we came. He didn't talk to us that day. Just lay in his bed with tubes going in and out of him, breathing heavily.

He doesn't talk. He sleeps a lot. He remembers things, says a few words.

What does he say? This is Krista, not me.

This and that. He says she was long-suffering and patient, he never deserved her.

Who was? I know, but Krista has to ask.

Your Paatiamma, ma, Esther. He is remembering your grandmother, now, when he is going to, to see her. My mother's voice breaks and I see she is on the verge of tears. She wipes her eyes, puts the watering-can down on the steps. She goes over to the balsam plant, stares without speaking into the deep orange flarings of the flowers.

He's going to see her?

Shush, I say, don't you know what that means?

Oh. Krista's eyes go round.

My mother is staring at the flowers as if the orange draws her deep into its center, enfolds and blinds her. She paces, fingering crotons in her hands, letting their long speckled leaves spill brown and red essences over her. She keeps doing this, back and forth, while we sit and pretend to string jasmine now, just watching her.

There is no calm in her face. She looks dazed.

But I think of the calm in Esther's face, the still, unspeaking eyes in her portrait. Maybe Esther's calm came from tasks like these. Planting, watering, sitting in the garden, looking deep into the heart of balsam flowers. Maybe she carried a lovely orange calm inside her, bright orange heart of balsam, incessantly budding and flowering. I catch myself in this thought. How could Esther be calm, when her husband refused to tell her the truth, to speak to her? How could she have been long-suffering and patient?

Again, I look up at her portrait before I go to my room. I think her eyes shimmer strangely at me. I look and look. I think I see a word in their depths, some kind of urgency in them. I tell myself I am imagining this, hurry on to our room. Krista is already in bed. I think I am beginning to imagine things now. Uneasily, I feel Esther's eyes upon me as I fall asleep.

Perhaps it is natural then, to dream of her. I dream she is in the garden with us, a slender woman in a pink silk saree, watering the balsams. Early morning light filters through leaves and spills around us. I am in the dream, watching her. Then I look at my hands and see a mirror there, her face in it. Calm gray eyes, closed-in face. It is surreal, in the way dreams are, one thing becoming another. I feel I am looking at Esther yet am Esther, myself. Slim, pink-saree-clad, staring into a mirror.

My image of Esther has changed. I had used to think of Esther as a wraith, insubstantial, used to giving in, to being moved sinuously through her life by her parents, husband, calm in her numerous assents. My mother's memories gave her to me as such: slight, diaphanous. But here I am, standing in sunlight, a mirror in my hands—a different kind of Esther. My Esther does not stay calm, but is taut, held-in, a great heap of anger inside her. She holds the mirror up to the street as if to see if Roderick is coming down it.

And I see the empty street in the mirror. A long street, crotons spilling over from people's houses into the street, which is not light but dark. A circle of streetlight shines in the middle, bright metallic white. I wait, but he does not appear. The second time I look I see Esther's face again, a lonely empty face. All the anger in me rises up then. I take my anger and make a fist of it, drive its clamped, withholding bud into my own reflected face, I shatter it. The harsh sound of the mirror falling, a metallic shock wave, reverberates into the garden. Shards of glass fly up and embed in my knuckles, in the mound of Venus on my palm, against my wrist. Behind me, the house is calm and unhearing, the house sleeps.

In the dream I look at the slow upwelling of blood in my skin, pieces of mirror scattering light at my feet. Balsam blood blooms on my fist, brightly, virulently orange. Each bead of blood a balsam flare, an empty room.

I wake abruptly to an ordinary night. Krista asleep beside me, dark leaves outside, a little breeze on my legs. Thoughts float upward: she must have felt rage, she let no one see it. All day she may have been calm, but she carried pain like a mirror's bruise inside her, its seven-year curse of misery wrapped in the breaking, hard, cold-edged, many years of it.

One afternoon that week it rained.

Afterward the rose bush hummed with butterflies, tiny and blue, they spun through leaves, backtracked, fluttered. Sun caught on the turquoise glass of their wings, hinged, expansive wings, constantly opening and closing as they trailed each other, flickered, rose.

Sumit said, Bet you can't catch one!

Reena and I had spent the afternoon painting. We came into the sun where Laila and Krista were playing, and the ocean I'd painted, blue, reared in a thunderous echo of wings around us. Enthralled, I brought my pencil out, began to sketch the scene: a rose, a clasp of leaves, hovering wings.

Catch one if you can!

I wouldn't *want* to, I said in disdain. Sky was in their wings, I thought, a powdery vivid blue, flicker of aqua, hint of ultramarine.

Sumit disappeared behind the steps. Reena looked over my shoulder as I drew.

I was halfway through the sketch when Sumit pushed the diamond-steeple of his closed hands against my arm, shrieked, let go, and wings rushed up against me, a ticklish, nervous fluttering. A flash of lucent blue stunned my eyes as the butterfly blew wind against my neck, trailed blindly up my cheek, twisted away.

It's nothing, he said, see, it flies! Before I could protest, he was doing it again, the butterflies were all over us, he caught them in seconds, dispersing their rain in a visceral pulsing of blue on skin.

I leapt up and ran after him, my papers flying, as if it were bees he'd brought to us, I was screaming as loudly as if I'd been stung. He flew around the side of the house, I pursued him. Round to the front of their house, into the street, directly in the path of my mother, obliged to leap aside twice as whirling dervishes struck. I should have known she would be home anytime soon. Sumit did an about-turn and vanished. I thought I'd go after him again but my mother stopped me, commandingly. *Elizabeth!*

Behind me, too late, Reena was giving out advice I should have taken: *just ignore him!*

At night my mother resumed her story as if it were playing out in her mind, she had to tell it, even if only to me, her recalcitrant daughter. One day her husband died and my father—she got up from the table and went into the kitchen to bring us the plate of aplums she'd left by the stove—my father took care of her.

I opened all the dishes on the table and peered in. Rice, sambar, fried vendaka, mango pickle, an omelette studded with green peas. What do you mean?

He gave her money, took care of her family. My mother raised her head and seemed to see me properly for the first time that night, playing with my food. Eat your omelette, Leeza!

The day the accident happened, Roderick was there, returning to his office from lunch. He saw the cement truck hurtle out of a side street on the wrong side of the road, saw the cart crush and break, guavas spilling blood as bags of cement broke open, metal bit deep into the man's lungs. He stopped, took the badly injured man to the government hospital at the other end of town.

He helped Suraiya later with the funeral expenses. He helped her get a small bank loan to buy a new cart, keep the business going. No one said a word when he began to visit her afterward. Not his mother to whom he gave most of his salary, month after month. Not his brothers, all younger than him, who had no voice to oppose him with. Not his father, senile, lost in his own memories. The family knew because Kanaka, who swept the garden and terrace every evening, lived down the street from Suraiya. Esther did not know what the family knew, because they took pains to keep it from her as if, always, she needed protection.

For a time, Esther appeared tranquil. After that first night, she would not question Roderick when he came home late, clothes crumpled, stain of liquor on his breath.

Very soon after the marriage, my mother said, she got pregnant. It was a good thing, because it took her mind off Roderick.

Now her stomach was swelling round and smooth so she could sit in the garden all evening, feeling its weight under her hands, listening for the feel of limbs.

It was also a bad thing, my mother said, because that must have been when she started to withdraw, more and more into herself. Those days when she looked at Roderick, she barely saw him.

The next morning Sumit showed me what he'd found, a red velvet beetle he'd locked inside a matchbox.

You have to let it go, I said, cringing at the thought of the creature being trapped, stroking the soft velvety back.

Do you know how hard it is to find one? He looked pained at my suggestion. You have to go out very early to see them. They disappear when the sun comes up.

The miniscule hunch of its back pulsed under my fingertip. It feels alive.

It *is* alive, silly, what do you think?

We stood side by side over the box, four o' clock sun gliding over us. I could hear Sumit's breathing, I did not speak. I thought I could hear his heart under my skin, beating.

Do you think he knows he's in a box, he asked at last.

I rolled my eyes. Wasn't he crawling about in the grass when you saw him?

Yes, that's true. He looked at me and made a rueful face. You're right, he must have learned by now he's trapped. He can't get to the grass, he must feel lost.

We went to the place where Sumit had found him, shook the box out. He lay, stunned for a moment in the grass. Then he began to quiver, as if sensing grass, earth, sky, wanting to move in all directions at once. I thought, as he moved, started to scuttle away, how Reena or Krista would never have conceded, the way Sumit had. I thought: how singular of him to call this anonymous beetle a "he." It made all the bones in my body lean trustingly toward him. My mother didn't believe girls could be friends with boys. Surely she would come to see, I thought, that Sumit is different.

That night we sat in the hall after dinner and watched lizards watch flying insects crowd against the fluorescent tube of light below Esther's portrait. It was a drizzly night, the light rain driving insects into the house. All kinds of insects, little ones, large ones, moths even. The whole family of lizards that lived behind Esther's portrait and in cracks in the wall in the veranda had come out and were eyeing their dinner with delight.

My mother was sorting through Esther's letters. I picked one up and opened it. There was a jumble of words all over the page. *Soul hidden*, Esther wrote, *time-darkened*.

She wrote to herself, my mother said. After the child came, all day, she was alone with the child.

Esther had parents then, and a brother. They lived in Coonoor, on her father's tea estate in the Nilgiris Hills, three hundred kilometers away. But these letters were tied together, addressed to no one, never posted.

He still stayed out in the evenings, my mother said. She could have taken a train, gone up there to Nilgiris. They came once to see the child, that was all. But she just kept living here. I still have the books she used to read. Thomas Hardy, Sir Walter Scott, Charles Dickens. She used to read. She must have been—my mother stopped and wiped her face with her pallu because she was crying now—she must have been lonely.

The letters were full of words run together as if in play, in random ways, and here and there a thought, a longing, a string of meaning.

Esther nursed her child. Named her child Mary. Mother of God, inviolable.

She slept in daylight, fitfully, interruptedly, and woke at night in the room's offerings of shadow and moon. She wrote, half-awake, sitting on the bed. She wrote to herself.

That night I dreamt a train, rushing through dark water. I looked out the window and saw rails that extended shakily on water and tore deeply to ocean, although I wanted them to rise, lead to my mother's hills. Expecting slopes lush with tea around us, I saw ocean instead, narrow beam of the Madras Harbor lighthouse all that shone about me. A red as deep as blood, it pulsed like a warning across my skin, it swung, returned, swung.

The train itself, corroded, incomplete, collapsed as it flew, pieces disintegrating. I was a part of the breaking, I clung to the sides of the train but they broke, water seeping, red, into the cabin. I could smell salt in the air, a hint of fish. Far in the distance I saw a trail of red, shiver of foam on the highest waves as they caught the beacon's eye and turned, turned to death and scarlet, bleeding.

Afterwards, sunlight.

I remember the day she found out about Suraiya, my mother said, because I was there. The servants must have talked to her. I was three years old. She took me with her and ran, the two of us, we almost disappeared forever from this house.

I remember she wore a violet saree.

I remember sunlight.

Late evening hands of light, long and tender on the grass, the woman, the child.

Esther lay in the grass of the park two streets away, near Mount Road, the busiest thoroughfare in the city, dust of the street on her skin, blouse, violet saree. Her child pressed close against her, mouth open in thirst, lips cracked and dark.

Esther's eyes were shut, the child's open. The child was watching the world: hands of sun through tamarind leaves, eddies of dust, rickshaws in the street, a cage full of tiny, forgotten birds huddled in the sun, silent. In the child's eyes: birds, and the deep, unremitting color of her mother's saree—violet.

They had lain all day in the grass. Roderick found them, lifted them, dusted them, engaged a rickshaw to bring them home. He found them only because when he'd gone home, his mother sent him out again, saying, Go find Esther. She'd never left the house before, alone, without him or his mother. He found her only because the mango vendor and the groundnut vendor told him where to find her. He took her home, put her in bed, handed the three-year-old to his mother for a feeding.

Then he left for the evening, imagining his world the same. Not wanting to be touched, or moved from the site of his desire.

But the shape of the earth had changed for Esther. Suddenly, irrevocably. What exactly had she seen, or felt, or heard? What did she know now, that it sat like gray stone in her eyes, and would not shift, lighten, lift?

Esther had learned about Suraiya from Kanaka.

The gate of the house was locked against her after that day because she was drawn to the street like a woman possessed. In its closure she sat on the steps of the house and looked through the bushes at the street, day after day, her child crying to speak to her, to be lifted, fed, loved.

The day's heat slow and loose and languorous on her skin. Her hands still, eyes empty. Her inability to care for Mary growing each day.

Roderick's mother took care of the child. In the days that followed, Roderick tried to reason with Esther. She was a mother, she had a daughter. Surely a mother needed to take care of her own child. Esther looked at him with her brilliant, vacant eyes, saying nothing, and no one could say really, looking at her, in that heightened inwardness she had embarked upon, that she saw him.

In those days, my mother said, she became as one possessed. She spoke to no one. She sat in the house all day and said nothing. I don't even know if she kept reading. She just helped with the cooking if someone asked her, mostly it seems she sat around doing nothing. She refused to take care of the child.

We'd been shelling groundnuts that my mother had roasted for us after dinner that night, as a special treat. My mother gathered up the pile of shells from the table and put them in a plate. Krista was eating as fast as she was cracking shells.

And who can blame her, my mother went on. My father never gave up Suraiya. He went to her house down the street every night.

It was one of the rare nights my mother told the story in front of Krista. Krista was listening just like Zorro, eyes wide and ears cocked, pausing in between crunching groundnut to listen.

She lived nearby?

Just down the street, my mother said. She had a small, one-roomed house. They say my mother went down there and saw it one night.

Who says? Krista didn't seem to know we could stop my mother with just one wrong question.

My mother looked up from groundnut shells. Luckily, she didn't seem to notice she was telling the story to Krista too. Oh everyone, she said. My mother-in-law, my aunts, my cousins, the servants. They say she went in the middle of the night and stood in the window and just stared down into the room. They say he woke up and saw her. It was a Full Moon night, the whole street must have been bright as daylight.

And in my dream that night is a blue as deep as midnight ink, and a house in it, a single room, with a window high above, moon round and whole inside. The room is Suraiya's, the house hers, but the only person within the room is Roderick. I think as I dream I am seeing the inside of Esther's mind. The walls are dark, an inky blue, thick with her absence. I think she must have come to see herself as this: opaque, obscuring, a darkness from which Roderick rose and walked, whole, into the shining of another woman's house, her single room.

They say she kept to her room for days afterward, my mother said, she wouldn't speak. It was like she could not recognize anyone anymore.

How simple it must have been, her world.

A pleating of hands, a braiding, incessant, of balsam shadow and light. Outside figures moved. They were hands, legs, eyes, they rose from the room's pillow-dark and lay back, rose and lay back, a brief foray, luminous, into form, a deep release, eclipsed, to sleep.

One evening, Reena's mother said, as our mother hovered at the door, waiting to collect us, Leeza was so quiet today! She and Sumit, all they did was play Chinese Checkers and read.

My mother, predictably, is not appeased by this. She attempts a smile she doesn't mean, they linger at the door talking briefly about my grandfather.

It is not right, she says to me as we leave, it is simply not proper, to spend so much time with a boy. You are young, you do not understand this.

Krista chimes in like a cuckoo clock: I'll tell Papa next time you talk to Sumit!

My mother says, yes, Krista, you do that, you keep an eye on her.

I look at them open-mouthed. I wish there were some way I could reassure her. Sumit's being a boy didn't warrant such caution. We were so much like each other. How will she respond, I wonder, if I tell her that? I consider the thought for a moment and desist. She may not take it the right way.

I think, she says, the next time I go out, I'll either take you with me or lock the door. No one will know you're inside, you'll be quite safe. It's high time you stopped going next door all the time!

He is just like Reena, I want to say to her. *Only more interesting.*

But I do not speak. We walk in silence to the point where their shrubbery gives way to ours, we step through and come to the back door. My mother opens the door, not looking at me. I step in ahead of her, go in the kitchen and pour myself water from a bottle in the fridge. I feel I should say something about Sumit now. Something slight and reassuring. But I seem to have lost my voice. I have no idea what to say.

That night my mother behaved as if there was no awkwardness between us and picked up the story of Esther again. What happened in those early years stained her forever, she said.

It was after dinner, we were sitting in the hall, Krista painting in her coloring-book, I trying to read the old copy of *The Last Mohican*

I'd unearthed among Esther's books in the hall cabinet. My mother was hand-stitching a pattern of red dahlias into a cream tablecloth for my grandfather's dining-room table.

For years my father had a double life. One inside the house with us, his mother, his family. The other life was secret, a second life with Suraiya. He never gave her up. My mother became a lonely woman, overnight, even though she lived with us.

I looked up at Esther's face in the portrait. That was her grief, I thought, looking at her eyes.

She became better in some ways, as I grew up. We went to the market, to Marina Beach, to the shops. But she also fell ill a lot. She became sick at a moment's notice. She kept to herself. She was always sad.

What happened to Suraiya?

She went away, to take care of her sick mother, she went back to her village, some ten years after my mother died. My mother did not have a normal life while she was alive. My father was never in the house in the evenings, for dinner, and he slept in the other house, with Suraiya, for many nights. They did not even go to church together, except on Easter, or Christmas.

Esther's eyes were not calm and still anymore as I looked. Just empty.

My mother looked up at her too. Pink is a joyful color, my mother said. That was not her own saree, in that picture. That was Roderick's mother's saree. I remember my mother mostly in dark sarees. She wore dark blue a lot, and maroon, and violet. In fact she had many sarees in shades of purple and violet. It was the color of her mind, she said, sighing, that was how she felt.

I like violet, said Krista. See! She was painting a beach scene predrawn for her in the coloring book. She had mixed blue and red on the page and violet watercolor was spreading thickly now over her ocean, sky, even sand.

Too much water, my mother said. Try to take away some of the water, Krista.

You should mix the paint in the palette, I advised. Not on the paper.

Krista gave me a daggers-drawn look. I'll do it the way I want, she said.

I've done it a hundred times before, I started, but my mother interrupted, hurriedly, Let her do it the way she wants! Just don't make your coloring book so wet, Krista!

My mother got up and went to the dining-room and came back with a piece of old towel she used to wipe the table with. Here, use this to blot off some of that water.

Krista took it, pointedly ignoring me.

Kanthi, old, stooped, thin as a bone, was in the house with us that night, eating her dinner outside the kitchen, in the backyard. She will sleep over a few nights, my mother said. Tomorrow I am going to spend the night at the nursing-home.

We looked at her, not knowing what to say, although Krista tried. Why, she said.

Your grandfather is very sick, my mother said. I don't know how long he has. She was very calm now, as if all the tears had dried up in her.

We stayed up a little longer. Then Kanthi came in and asked where she should sleep.

Right here, said my mother, getting up. Come, Leeza, Krista, time for bed.

We helped her put a mat and blanket and pillows down on the hall floor for Kanthi. Then we went to bed.

Silence drowns me as I sleep, drowns me in violet. We are at Marina Beach, which has become Krista's painted beach, there's chaos at that boundary of red and blue, wild drenching of water, streamers of red floating to sky to birth violet. The walls of Esther's room are ground to pieces here, the slow revolving moon, grief that stole upward through her veins, streamed into her breath, bones, heart. The quiet that lay under her skin turned intensely to violet.

Sumit is in the dream, as too is my mother. Sumit is standing on the shore, far in the distance. I am floundering in the water because I don't know how to swim. On top of the water floats my mother. A violet house beside her, and a giant lock. She is trying to grab me, push me inside the house. But the bobbing violet waves separate us. *Help*, I want to shout to Sumit, *Help, Help!* But he cannot save me. He is too far. He could never hear me. I look across and my mother is closer, the bobbing house and lock are closer. My mother could save me. I try to shout, but my voice fails me. Nothing comes out when I try, but a squeak, too easily drowned by the thunderous roar of the ocean.

I look across and see Esther's eyes, gray and quiet, staring into a violet room. I know I am going to drown then. I see death approach in the dream, know how the muteness of my voice has turned against me. The whole ocean violet. Such a deep unremitting color. Such a clustering of grape at the surface. Such refusal to rouse itself from that painful depth, turn, lighten, shift.

Is it an ocean or an empty room? Sonorous, stubborn, bitter. Above us, the full moon shines, bright and white. But I cannot wake, break through these walls of violet. They cover, choke me. Flow over, bathe me.

Sumit has disappeared. My mother has disappeared. Violet then the skin, the bone of me. Violet, my terrible, flaying destiny. I am mostly underwater, although I try to gasp, choke, come up for air, kick my legs out in some futile attempt to swim. Seaweed waves up to my face, wraps around me. I am doomed, I think, forever to this violet sea, garlands of purple weed at my throat, violet limbs entwined with mine, virulent stain upon my thighs, white-moon aching. Never to lift or breathe transparent air again. Never to turn, look backward to the shore, return to my beginning-place. Never to wake.

To drown instead, in this viscous shroud of violet.

A slow dying.

That is what my mother calls it, a slow dying.

My grandfather Roderick is fastened by one lung to the world, one sack's weight of churning, returning air, the other lost over years to cancer. His eyes lie asleep on his breathing. Saline and dextrose fed to his veins, oxygen, clean and sharp, into his lung.

By his bedside, Mary, my mother, keeps vigil. It is the second night she has slept over at the nursing-home, the night after I dream the drowning.

Click Clack.

I listen to wind in the high dark and hear how Esther moves above my head on the mango terrace, knocking her heels on wind. It is after midnight. Upstairs the dogs stop their crying and start to bark, loud forceful barks of protest.

Esther's steps are firm, they seem complete. For every memory of her silence in those long years of her grief, I think, now each high-heeled step is a word released, a voiced dissent, a voice against sleep.

I have known Roderick only as brooder, sifter of thoughts, reclusive night-wanderer in the house's long corridors. The grandfather who lived by himself in his father's house, refusing to leave. Who survived his wife's premature death at thirty-four by turning abruptly to religion. Who proved his innate dislike of all things familial by leaving the raising of his child to his mother.

Whose house, in which we sleep, calls tonight for her, as if to a living presence whose hands are familiar against the room's every sleeping cheek, tender nape, the early-swelling, ever-beating heart.

I lie in the moon's traversing of the sheets, the dogs' pained uneasy breath. I hear the exact moment of his dying. Not as sound, but its absence. Lulling of wind in high trees, slow burn of star over mango leaves and cloud-lift, new depth of watery blue opening in a distant sky. A holding, inward, of the breath, pause in a woman's wood-heeled step on brick. The dogs abruptly silent.

The window is open. A very slight breeze blows across the windowbars, enters.

I feel strangely certain I will never hear Esther again.

I remember birds, my mother said.

They were everywhere. All day, wrecked by sun, crouching deep in the shadow of that cage, retreating from the sudden grasp of hands. They were speaking to each other. I saw only that fluttering, the beat of sun on wing, on beak, on their speech.

They were birds from the forests at the foothills of the Eastern Ghats, which is eight hours' journey by train from home, birds stolen from the naked trees, birds trapped and caged. They lived where Esther had lived once, in the Nilgiri hills. Song birds. Infant birds. Crying, fear-pecked birds. A crowd of dusty, brown-winged, honey-songed birds left in a cage by the side of a road.

When I cried, they looked at me.

The house filled overnight with people. A hearse came fom the hospital, bearing the body. When I looked where my grandfather had used to be, I saw only a memory of his body. A disappearing, a shell: white-haired, ascetic, a body laid out in an open coffin. Death's humid scent in the room, death and roses.

I ran out into the garden, the dazzle, persisting of sun.

Overnight, our summer had ended. The limewashed wall shone with it, the balsam's fading orange. The garden lay unswept, I waded through a strewing of dry leaves from the mango. I had overheard telephone conversations: my father would arrive, arrange for the funeral. The house to be closed, perhaps later to be rented. We were going to leave. My father's mother in Bangalore, diabetic, requiring dietary attention, needed us, or more accurately, my mother.

When my mother came in that morning, looking glazed, exhausted, she said to me: I saw my mother at the hospital. She came through the wall. She was there for him at the end, to help him through. I am sure he saw her. He looked up just before he closed his eyes.

What was she wearing?

I don't remember. Something pale, like mother-of-pearl. Shining.

Why, I said, frowning. Why would she help him through?

My mother wiped her eyes with her pallu. Sometimes it's not what happens to us from the outside that defines us, she said. Sometimes it's what is inside us that makes us go on. She never stopped wanting her life, she said. She never stopped caring for my father.

He didn't deserve her caring, I observed, coldly. He was creepy to her.

Her life revolved around her marriage, my mother said. But her marriage never really began. And she wanted it.

It was a hot June morning. I looked at the bright sunlight everywhere, on the walls, the leaves, the red earth. The shoeflower bush by Reena's house still in the heat, in stupor. Roses on the red-rose bush had started to lose more of their petals. The remnants of roses white and pink in the heat. On the circle of dry leaves below I saw the white face of sun reach down and burn leaves to a shred.

Sumit stood beside the rose-bush, pulling bleakly on his harmonica. Is your grandfather dead?

I nodded. We're leaving, I said.

Back to Bangalore?

Yes. By the end of the week.

A small ribbony wind blew down on us. Sea-wind, I thought, blowing all the way from Marina Beach, remembering my dream of the early morning, while my grandfather lay in the new cocoon of his death. The ocean blue. Faint, the stillness of green in far water. Morning hues.

Was it the dream Esther gave me as she left? I dreamt of beach and water again, dreamt I learned to swim, ocean blue and green about me. No hint of violet. The waves foam-lit, buoyant. I dreamt I saw the line of shore, voice of return etched on a blue ocean. I turned and swam in the soft seablue out to the vast expanse. Toward layers of morning turquoise water, new continent under a sunlit sky.

I'll give you my address, Sumit offered. You can write to me!

I looked at him, speechless. For precisely a second. You write first, I'll write back, I said.

He grinned. Did you ever finish that sketch?

A wall broke, a feeling surged, a handful of butterflies rose shimmering and live inside my mind.

Elizabeth! Around the side of the house, my mother approached. Panic in her voice, white lace and locked doors, anxious to stave off lightning. She must have seen us through the window. She must have been watching us.

I'll send it to you, I said. You can frame it and hang it on your wall!

She came up to where we stood. I want you to look for the candles, she said, inventing an errand on the spot. The white candles, and the prayer books. Didn't you hear me calling you, Elizabeth?
She appeared not to be able to see Sumit. He was crouched, pulling dead flowers off the bush. Behind him I saw the host of blue wings, the fluttering. Sumit flicked a dry shoeflower at me. I picked up a pink rose-petal from the ground and flicked it back at him.

I'm coming, I said, to my mother, brushing petals away from my hair. *Don't panic.*

The Couple in the Park

꠵ For three weeks now, she had watched them. From where she sat, in the steel folding-chair by the window, she could see through the partial overhang of trees to the stone bench in the Ganesha park three stories below.

Here was the back of the building, and here the high concrete wall (once a delicate shade of gray, now wind-washed and weather-stained, crowned with jagged bits of glass) that separated Mudra Apartments from the park behind it. The glass, entrenched in the sloped concrete with pieces of metal and broken ends of barbed wire, was meant to preserve residents from intruders, but she knew no one in the building felt protected by it; there had been break-ins before, things lost, things stolen, and a building guarded by a single watchman, now in his sixties and not very light on his feet, could barely pose a threat to an ambitious intruder. It seemed as if the owners doubted the efficacy of the security systems available on the market, for they disdained to install one; the tenants, after a series of petitions and complaints, Lionel included, must have decided very soon that they had expended sufficient energy on the cause, for they gave up and began to accept the situation with remarkable composure. Few of them ventured to install combination locks and chains of their own; this part of Madras was after all older, quieter, a lower-middle-class neighborhood, no glitzy motorbikes, no flashy cars, and security was expensive.

She could not tell how old they were—mid-sixties, early seventies perhaps—but they were fairly agile for their age. The man dressed invariably in gray trousers and a loose white shirt; the woman wore unstarched cotton sarees in discreet shades that did not typify her presence so much as mute her into dusk, the lengthening shadows, the heavy trees. Laura had decided they were cotton sarees, although, from this height, she could have been mistaken, they could have been crepe or nylon, not starched, that was all, as hers were (crisp and shapely), but draped rather shabbily on the woman's thin figure, looking rather like the thin Kanchi cottons her grandmother had used to wear when she was alive.

They came early to the park, just when school was letting out and the sun turning to gold on the grass and the children home from school, knocking decorously on the door to be let in. Laura would shuffle to her feet, put her sewing aside and open the door for them. They didn't fly in as the other children in the colony did. They smiled tentatively at her and slid in, cautious and gentle, as if resolved not to disrupt the afternoon silence of the house. This small courtesy to the sleeping house, like all the others (built up over the years and so ingrained now that no one in the house could imagine an alternative) was taken for granted. Laura certainly never questioned it. These were Lionel's children. And this was Lionel's house.

In his own father's house, Laura knew, Lionel, youngest son of his parents, had stood quietly on the outskirts of things. Now oddly enough, as a consequence of time perhaps, a consequence of his perceived *manhood*, perhaps, at family gatherings, his voice was welcomed, sought after, yet when he was growing up, his three sisters and six brothers had always come before him. Laura knew this because she had seen the family photographs, heavy black and white imprints of the nine children, and the parents who looked younger but as severe, his father standing straight and tall in the studio with the simulated backdrop of stormy ocean behind him, posture matching his impeccable British clothing, a white crescent moon affectedly slicing his left ear, eyes like slit diamonds looking resolutely into the narrow pinhole of the camera, so that they focused, hard and unswerving, on her face as she thumbed through the pages of the album. In these pictures, meticulously posed and taken at the same studio every two years, all through their growing-up, their faces thinning, extending, changing, Lionel was made to stand at the very end of the long row of younger children, and in some of the photographs, you could see how his face was half-turned toward his father, his body tense, hands bunched into little fists.

It was no secret after all that Lionel's father was a strict man, he ruled his household with *a rod of iron* as Lionel used to say, faintly rueful, half-joking, for he fostered an inexplicable devotion (bred peculiarly of fear and love) for his father, and thought at any rate that he was the most *correct* person in the world. Propriety was paramount. The family was raised, as was Laura's own family, well within all the proper constraints of society, to respect always the correct thing to do and the correct way of doing a thing. But when Lionel was in his teens, he entered, involuntarily, into the complicity of malehood; unlike his sisters, he was then allowed to ride his brother's motorbike, to eat out at restaurants with his friends, to go to movies, and to return home as late as he wished. Another world opened then to him, a world outside the family, and he found his father surprisingly amenable to his exploits.

Boys, his father would say, affectionately, a sentiment easily transferred to his impressionable son, so easily that Laura would often hear Lionel say of their own eldest son Robert, in joyful (but private) celebration of his sex, boys will be boys!

Laura sensed, after having lived in Lionel's father's house for many years after their marriage, and seeing how they lived, that Lionel believed he could not *be* Lionel without, paradoxically, becoming his father. But this was a knowing she kept secret, and learned to live with.

Tea-time. Snacks—murukus, bhajis, bondas, vadais—that she sometimes spent whole afternoons preparing. Milk for the children, tea for her. Play-time. The children were allowed one hour to themselves before they began their homework. The girls stayed in their room, playing with their dolls. The boy, who was now ten, would beg to be allowed out to play with the other boys in the building. Cricket or marbles in the narrow sanded area in front of the building. Or flying kites in the park. Laura would let him go. Boys will be boys, she would tell herself. But she would wait anxiously by the door till he came back, ten minutes to the hour. It was sacred, the unspoken agreement between them. His father should never see him down there.

Lately, Laura herself had taken to spending this time, the children's play-time, by the dining-room window. The couple did not do much. They sat there on the bench, ostensibly watching the children play. There were always children in the park. In the evenings, anyway. Laura would look at the tiny figures below playing hide-and-seek and pandi and catchball, she followed the twist and turn of their running figures with absorption. Their voices carried clearly up to her, their laughter and shouting tearing open the quiet that hung over this forgotten part of Robinson Road, where their building, although ten years old, was still considered "new," and, in the view of long-term residents of this area, a disfiguring blot on a perfectly proportioned (house and garden, stop, house and garden) landscape.

From the girls' bedroom, there was barely a rustle to be heard. To Laura, this was normal. Play-time meant noise from below and outside. Everything was different up here.

Six o'clock. Lionel would arrive, as immaculate in his neatly-pressed shirt and perfectly-tied tie and stiffly-creased trousers as when he had left. She would put away his briefcase, bring him fresh hot tea, the newspaper. The children would sit at the table with their books. Study-time was when the silence became absolute.

When she had finished cooking, Laura, her back to the shuttered window, would lean over the tablecloth or dress or blouse she was sewing and breathe as quietly as she could. The merest shiver of a child's hand on paper lifted and hung in the air. In that silence, the arrhythmic scrape of their pens and the rustle of Lionel's newspaper became large and distinctive. An hour, two. The children would shift their work to their rooms. Lionel watched the eight o'clock news on the small black-and-white in the parlor. Laura set the table for dinner.

Just before she called them in, she would push aside the bright flowered curtains, unfasten the shutter, and look out. It was hard to see anything very clearly, standing as she stood in the sterile whiteness of the room's fluorescent light, but she'd lean close to the rusting bars and narrow her eyes. The street lamps would be on, and the few lights in the park. There they would be, just rising to go, two meager silhouettes in that pared yellow light, walking close together, away from the bench and into the trees. Then Lionel would call, Isn't dinner ready yet? and she would, quickly, carefully, draw the shutter in, latch it, pull the curtains to and call back, Yes! Dinner's ready.

She didn't know who they were. They didn't live in the building, she was certain of that. She never saw them in the street, in the market, at the post-office. She never saw them anywhere except in the park. She wondered about them sometimes. Did they have children? Grandchildren? Perhaps one child, she'd think. He was married and lived in Bombay. His wife didn't get on very well with his mother. He worked in a bank, like Lionel, and he liked his work. Like Lionel, he had three children and a dog. No, she'd correct herself, no dog. Now why did I think of that, a dog? Lionel would never have a dog.

Each time this happened, when some quirk in her own imagination caught her unawares (usually at dinner-time), she would look up to find Lionel looking curiously at her.

You're smiling, he'd say. What are you smiling about?

She'd flush under his scrutiny, her light skin reddening. Nothing, she'd say. Nothing. Was I smiling? Do you want some more rice?

Have you finished the children's uniforms yet? he'd ask, and she would flush again, guiltily. It was hard to get work done these days. Almost, she would say, almost, and get up quickly, and fetch ice from the refrigerator or hurry into the kitchen for more rice.

This Wednesday evening was like all the others, she thought, her eyes on the couple in the park, hands still in her lap. Children were playing. The girls were in their room. The smell of potatoes frying wafted in; the family downstairs was making dinner. But there was something different about the scene. She couldn't put her finger on it.

She put the silver spoon she was polishing with soap powder down on the flat, wooden ledge of her Usha sewing machine and leaned closer to the window. The hot white smell of bleach rose into her nostrils. She rose and put the spoons away and tucked the bleach beside the sink in the kitchen. Then she came back, picked up the dated *Woman's Own* she had borrowed a long time ago from the library, and sat down by the window.

It looked the same: dry, dust-coated leaves of the mango tree shifting in a small breeze, grass browning in the lengthening light, children skipping rope near the sandpit; in the distance the boys playing cricket, and there, in that small clearing, cool oasis of the stone bench, and the couple. They were in the forefront of her vision, as always; the trees and the laughter and the playing rested, meagerly, in the periphery of her regard. She wondered why she could not locate it, this niggling difference in the small panorama laid out before her in almost perfect replay of the evenings before. Perhaps I'm imagining it, she thought. I shall look away for a minute and look back and it will be gone. Nothing could have changed from yesterday, could it? So she looked away for a second, shifting focus to the sandpit and the swinging arms of the girls at either end of the rope, the great, tautened arc as it swept the air sharply, whipping faint clouds of dust with it, the children in the center jumping up and down, up and down, and she looked back again at the center, the bench, the couple, and she knew immediately what it was.

They were *talking* to each other.

On other days, she was certain, they had simply sat there, like her grandparents had used to, in front of their house, watching the children play.

They never spoke. Not to each other.

Sometimes her grandmother would call to her as she pulled twigs from the bougainvillea, dragging her doll in the dirt, and she would look questioningly at them as they sat there, quiet and distant, a thin smile cracking the rigid lines of her grandfather's face, and she would hold the ends of the lowest, thorn-backed branch in her chubby five-year-old fingers and shake it at them, ungently, awkwardly, smiling all the time, until her grandmother came to her and loosened that resolute grip, pulling the doll from her hands, straightening its clothes, its hair, while she stood, suddenly mute, rain of dry petals at her feet.

This vision had stayed with her, she realized, running like a fine undercurrent through her mind while she watched the couple come and take their places on the bench and sit through dusk, unmoving and silent. It had been fitting somehow, the passive quiet between them, tremulous echo of all those evenings in the garden, settled complacency of that quiet, her grandparents never saying a word to each other, content merely to measure the falling of dusk in sleepy bird-call and the beginning whir of crickets and the smell of cooking in the air and the sound of returning feet beating a steady tattoo on the street outside.

Something in the way they came, unobtrusive, unselfconscious, into the small circle of her awareness and halted there, for an hour, two hours, in that unforced fidelity to her own opaque expectations, had been calming to her, and soothing, and uplifting. As if they were, without desire to mimic, submitting to a timeless impulse, re-living an old memory locked inside her.

It was a violation of all that was natural that they should speak to each other.

She tried to imagine their conversation and could not. The man was turned sideways in his seat, knees crossed toward her, head tilted. The woman's saree billowed slightly in the breeze, and she put one hand down to tether the lifting pleats, gesticulating with the other. Laura wished she could hear her. After weeks of silence, the suddenness of their discourse came as an incongruity into her world.

Her grandparents had always been that way—*closed to each other*, she realized, yet the quiet in the house had been heightened by her father's death.

It was an accident, a boating excursion on the river in Coimbatore at the wrong time of year, a drowning no one could have foreseen or averted. Laura could still hear their voices echoing like cool metallic bells in the open vault of the hallway, her mother shrinking in tears as his body was brought in, dripping on the floor, his two friends, big burly men of otherwise stable disposition, shaking as they stood there after laying him down, shaking just looking at him. We were lucky to find his body downriver, they said. There were rocks and trees.

You let him go, her grandmother was saying, over and over, Why did you let him go? and her grandfather, so much like Lionel's father, upright tea-estate manager, perennial excuser of boyish high spirits, encourager of wild, verging-on-danger exploits, stood there, not saying a word, simply looking at the flaccid, bloated body of his son, until something must have broken in him for he caught her by the shoulders and looked in her eyes and said, You couldn't have stopped this from happening, this was his time, his fate, fiercely, decisively, as if the utterance of it should, in some conclusive way, thwart and forestall the grief that allowed for no closing of doors in its face but came, impervious and heavy, settling into dust in every cranny of the house.

It was a calamity, a loss, a terrible end they never recovered from, either of them, although they put a calm face on it and were always civil to each other, especially in company, projecting a willingness to listen that fell away in private, in their determined retreat to their separate lives, until there they were, in front of their grand-children, side by side on the bench in the garden, with nothing to say to each other, not a word.

And now to see them talking to each other like that, casually, close-ly, as if they had been doing it all their lives, as if the previous si-lence between them had been mere play, a pretence, was such a jolt to her, such a shaking of the scene in her mind that she sat there, staring at them, forgetting the magazine she held loosely in her hands, forgetting the time ticking away on the black pendulum clock that hung, austere, watchful, in the dining-room, not notic-ing the color of the grass, how it deepened to bronze and began to fade, or the shadows, starting to shift uneasily about the trees, not seeing the girls as they ran out of their room, rushing to open the front door for Robert and their father. Not aware they were stand-ing there, looking at her, all of them, Lionel and the children, not realizing there was anything wrong even as she turned around and saw them, stopped as if bewildered, uncertain, stopped in the se-curity of that routine they had made their own, registering only as pale, cut-out figures in her mind.

What's wrong with you? Lionel wanted to know, crossing to where she sat, and peering into the dusk. What are you staring at?

She sat very still and the children came quietly up to her and stood beside her. Lisa, the youngest, picked up the magazine that had fallen to the floor and handed it to her and she smiled and took it, not thinking very much at all, feeling no desire to move.

What's wrong with you? Lionel's voice was rising, as if he couldn't help himself. What's going on here?

She smiled up at him, beatifically, serenely, and said nothing at all, and he put his briefcase on the table and felt her forehead, her throat, her hands, and frowned to himself.

Is Mummy ill? asked Robert, not daring to come nearer, hover-ing in the doorway, looking tense and worried. He had knocked, timidly, desperately, frenetically, and the girls had run to the door, but his father had arrived just then, and seen him standing there.

You go to your room! snapped Lionel, I'll deal with you later, not addressing his query at all, fumbling for an answer himself.

What's wrong with you? he said again to her, forcefully, violently, in the way he sometimes spoke to the children the day they brought their report cards home and he examined them, meticulously, subject by subject, demanding their attention. What's happened? Laura, say something!

You're early today, she said, and it was instantaneous, she could see his face clearing, his body almost visibly relaxing.

No, I'm not, you're behaving very strangely today. Where's my tea?

The sharp note of concern had dropped flatly to censure, and as if from a dream she had been fighting against all day but was slowly waking from, unbalanced, unsure of her bearings, she lifted herself from the chair and went to the kitchen, she opened the small cabinet over the sink, removing cups, saucers, a spoon. When she came back to the dining-room with sweet tea in her hands, steaming and fresh, Lionel had already settled in with his newspaper and gave her no more than a cursory, frown-filled glance as he took it.

Something changed in the house after that, for it seemed to Laura the children were always about her, solicitous, eager to help, bending over her mornings when she woke, clustering ineffectually about her evenings when they came in and found her reluctant to abandon her seat by the window; she returned to it as if it were in some way a refuge—from what neither she nor her family could comprehend. It seemed that she had slipped without her own knowledge away from the time-bound and ordered reality of their existence; all that afforded solace of a kind was the iron-barred, leaf-obstructed view from that window, which, now open throughout the day, let in wind and dust and dried, curling leaves that came piecemeal and broken through the bars to rest on the table, chairs, the floor. She would sit for hours until the sun began to slide from its white-hot seat at the top of the sky and begin to lose its heavy, torpid heat, sending shadows of trees in long pencils of brown dark to pattern the grass; each day the slow meandering sunlight prepared her for the small rush of emotion that assailed her when the couple came in, nonchalant but orderly in that disciplined return, taking their places on the bench, letting the dark fall about them. It was hard, afterward, to divorce that lucent image from the ones in her mind; they came at her like swiftly falling leaves and merged indissolubly into each other, until she was brought into the garden again, and the laughter calling upward from the park became her own, and the candor in the couple's posture as they sat, smiling, talking, suffused the distance between her grandparents and brought them closer together.

There was a photograph, faded and yellowing but framed, hung on the wall behind her bed, along with the posed studio shot of her wedding and pictures of the children, that began, at this time, to provoke her attention, drawing her into the garden as if she were there now, a part of the sunlight falling, slanted and light on her grandfather's house as he stood, a little apart from her grandmother, her face open and smiling, shyly, selfconsciously, as if deprecating that sudden, deliberate focus on her. She would wander into the room and sit at the foot of her bed and stare at it, recalling the long summer afternoons when she tried to read or draw while her mother slept beside her, and her grandmother moved noiselessly around the house, dusting every trophy her father had won in long-ago cricket and hockey tournaments, every ornament in the living-room—brass or copper or wood—that rested forever in the one place it had been assigned, inside the glass-fronted cabinets set in the wall. Her grandmother never liked to be disturbed during this time; her face, intent and serious, would scrunch up into a frown if Laura entered the living-room. Laura would let the folds of the curtain fall about her as she peeked around it. It was difficult, then, simply to sit still while the hours sounded in the slow metallic chimes of the old clock and passed away.

Once, at dinner, she tried talking to Lionel about it, thinking restlessly in turn of the couple in the park and the picture in her mind as she ate, until she could keep it to herself no longer and she said, to Lionel, You've seen them too, haven't you? That woman, she reminds me of my grandmother. Don't you think she's like her?

There fell a bleak, remorseless silence in which Lionel looked blankly at her, and the children, suddenly uncomfortable, shuffled in their seats. Carol asked for water and the moment passed, but Laura felt cheated somehow, as if they were withholding something from her, telling her she must handle this acuity of perception on her own.

Sometimes, watching them where they sat, wind blowing lightly through the trees, she would be filled with a quiet excitement, that built inside her so that she would attempt, evening after evening, to reinvent that ease she sensed there in the park inside, in her own household, each time coming up against this wall her family held so firmly in front of her, as if deliberately, unkindly, ranging themselves against her, implacable, unresponsive, blank.

The months slid by and summer waned in the slow gathering of clouds overhead, the first tentative drops of the monsoon. It rained intermittently at first, wind blowing wet-earth fragrance into the room, and then the monsoon strengthened and quickened, rain came heavy and blinding, sweeping sharply in through the window and collecting in pools on the floor, until Lionel, in desperation, boarded up the window and latched the shutter tightly shut, and she could not, in her repeated and frail attempts, unlatch it, push it open.

She tried, at first, for days, the rust of the latch did not yield although she pulled the little trigger as hard as she could with sweating fingers. She pushed then, unreasonably, at the shutter, despite the latch, and of course it did not budge, although the wood almost cracked under the pressure of her hands. The girls saw her one afternoon and came up to help her, but their efforts were more puny than her own and as unsuccessful. They were watchful though, they saw her distress and strove to distract her, first with requests for special sweets for tea and then persuading her, slowly, to take them to the new children's library near the post-office, in between rain storms, all three of them leaping over puddles in the middle of the street, Laura's saree-hems trailing in mud and inevitably getting wet. In the afternoons now they stopped going into their room but sat in the dining-room beside her, idly talking, doing their homework, painting in their painting-book, keeping an eye on her while she sewed, or read a magazine, or just sat in her chair, staring at the closed window.

For a while this seemed to help, but then Laura began to rise when the children approached and go by herself into the bedroom and lock the door. They were uneasy at first and tried to bring her back to the dining-room, but Laura was used to being alone for a while after they came home, and ignored their gentle knocks on the door. Go away, I'm sleeping, she would call, although she wasn't, and the girls would wait a few moments, then retreat. After a few days of this, they did not knock when she left for her room, they retreated, themselves, to theirs.

In the daytime she was alone, as always. But whatever it was, she thought, that had changed in the house had begun to wreak its own change in her, she was slowly becoming less comfortable with being alone. She did not know why at first, but then she noticed the change in her surroundings.

She did not say anything to Lionel when it first began to happen, the footsteps that she heard, during the daytime, heavy and rhythmic on the common corridor outside the apartment; she would check the bolts on the front door and lock the bedroom door and sit inside, shaking, eyes fixed on the door as if any moment now it would open, slowly at first, almost invisibly, and he would enter the room, this unnamed intruder who walked incessantly up and down the corridor outside. It never happened; the door remained shut and unmoving, but this did not mean it never would. Laura felt that if she did not keep her eyes on the door, always wide-open, always aware, it would yield to the force waiting outside and swing open on its own; she could not keep this pervasive unease from the children in the afternoons, and they told their father, repeatedly, expectantly, so that, disbelieving, annoyed, he put in a new lock on the front door and a bar across it with a little chain secured to the wall so that no one could enter if they were not welcome and she would always feel protected.

But she did not. She continued to lock herself in the bedroom, keeping her watch on the door, convinced that someone knew, someone was watching, in malice and eagerness, that this was her portion now, this having to keep watch, in sickening fear but full awareness, senses sharply alive.

It was during this time also that she began to hear the faint whispering in the room, the steady, sinuous insertion of voices into the silence until the quiet became peopled with a sibilance rushing tangentially at her from the walls, voices that she could, at first, neither identify nor locate.

Later she wondered why she had doubted their existence. Sitting on the bed, she would look at the picture. She thought she could recognize the voices. They were her own. They were her parents', her grandparents'. But it was confusing. They were both inside her and outside her. She wondered first if she was hearing the voices of the dead speak to her. Then she wondered if the voices, long suppressed inside her, had taken on a vocal life *outside of her own being* and were projecting themselves at her from the outside, from the walls, the room, the window. She had certainly endured various suppressions of her own voice. Decorum, her grandmother would say, a girl must always have that. *Self-control*—no running into the house like that, shouting so loudly for your mother!

It became surprisingly easy to slip backward in memory then to the moment that lay like pooling water in the back of her mind, cool and silent water, not rippling but stagnant, a night-pool, very still. She was fourteen, in high school. The year 1959. Her mother had used to listen as if receptive when she talked about wanting to go to medical college and taking science in Intermediate, but her grandfather's response was markedly different. The first time he got to hear of it he didn't say anything, not immediately. It was a Sunday morning and they were in her grandfather's car, on their way to church. He turned and looked at her curiously, as if he had never seen her before.

Her grandmother spoke sharply to her mother. I hope you

haven't been putting ideas into her head, she said. No respectable mother would send her child to a co-ed college. She gave the word co-ed a sinister emphasis and directed a withering glance at Laura.

Her grandfather spoke. That's not the only thing, he said, slowing to make a turn. She must think about getting married.

Her grandmother looked annoyed. She liked to believe she had thought of everything first. We've talked about this before, haven't we, Lillian? School is probably a bad influence on her—wanting to become a doctor indeed!

Her mother had never mentioned marriage before. Besides, she wasn't in the habit of talking about things with her mother-in-law. Laura sat crouched in her seat, starched cotton blouse she was wearing biting into her.

You don't understand, she said suddenly. It's what I want to do, don't you see? Why, I could look after you when I got my degree! You wouldn't have to worry about me—don't you see? I could have a practice of my own!

She had never said the words before, not out loud, not to her grandparents, never to anyone but her mother, and it was such perfect release now to let the words out, she said them again, this Friday afternoon, listening as they broke through the clamor of voices coming at her, and then again, into the silence, breaking it, beating it down, with sudden power in her voice.

Someone came into the room then, and she knew it, she could feel them there, standing behind her, looking at her. Was it the intruder, waiting always by the door, listening to her breathe? *But she was no longer afraid.* It was as if she had come up against something in herself that she didn't know she had, it was strong and it would keep her safe. And she turned her head, calmly, defiantly; it was Lionel. There was someone standing beside him whom she did not recognize, and when he came forward and took her hand, she let him do it, not resisting, not thinking very much anymore, just sitting there, letting him stroke something soft and wet on her arm. She put her other hand up to stop the sudden sting and she pushed his hands away but something was happening to her, she could not decipher what. She closed her eyes and lay back on the bed.

When she woke, thin light from a half-hidden sun was streaming into the room. Lisa and Carol and Robert were sitting on the bed and looking at her.

You should be in school, she said, confused.

Mommy, it's Saturday, said Robert.

Did you just come back? she asked. She got up and went to the door.

Mommy. It's Saturday *morning*.

You're home early, she said. Carol would not look at her. Lisa was crying.

She walked into the dining-room toward the window. The window was open. The shutter pulled back, morning sunlight flooding into the room. The sky was no longer gray and filled with rain-clouds but a soft watercolor blue. She looked down, down where the park was, and the empty bench, and the patterns of sunlight through the trees. She looked up, she saw them. They were standing by the dining-room table, expressions of sadness on their faces. They were dressed in white, as she had always seen them. Cotton, she saw. Exactly as she had thought. Funny, she thought, they look exactly like my grandmother and grandfather. She stared at them. They *were* her grandparents, she realized. Every day they had come there, sitting on that bench like neon signs and yes, she had felt that sameness about it, that sense of knowing, yet she had never truly been *certain*.

They came toward her in the sunlight and she let them, watching the way the uncrisped cotton fell limply about the woman's figure, the way the lines on the man's face stretched and changed when he smiled. She put out a hand, as if in welcome, and they touched her.

Outside, the clouds moved across the sun and the wind began in the trees.

The Man on the Veranda

ॐ He was a clerk in a government office in a small town in Tamil Nadu until he retired. When that occurred, he was a few months short of sixty and combed his graying hair horizontally across his scalp. His wife had taken to covering her head all the time, even inside the house, with the pallu of her saree, so that it looked always as if she were on the verge of prayer. You could say they were trying in their own way to conceal their age, although they told themselves it was wisdom they were acquiring.

Parameswaran had begun to think about this a lot lately, how it was all a matter of perspective. These mornings he sat on the stone veranda with a book in his hands and no desire to open it. The people in the street passed by and he looked at them. It was altogether a pleasant pastime because the street was beyond the gate and the gate made of vertical iron bars that let the street in, yet could be locked firmly against it. The people came and went. Parameswaran had concluded it was most diverting because he did not work for them. Not one of them paused to inflict on him the latest episode in their life story or demand his agreement with all their insipid opinions. This was gratifying. To add, not one of them lingered. Perhaps for a moment, yes; there were always those who looked up from their meandering thoughts or duties and returned the half-blank, half-curious stare Parameswaran bestowed on the world. But not for long, not even the most hardened and vacuous among them. Clearly, thought Parameswaran, they all tired of him before he tired of them. And that was fine with him.

One Monday morning when the heat had begun especially early and had settled close in the cracks between his toes and thin fingers, Parameswaran looked up briefly from his ongoing meditation on life in general and his in particular, something that often put him in a kind of trance where he blissfully erased his surroundings, and observed, much to his comfort, that he was sitting on the veranda as usual. It was perhaps too hot to have been sitting out there all this time, wind dead in the trees and summer a flat heavy hand on his face. But there he was, legs crossed at the ankles, leaning back in his easy-chair and turned toward the benign street as usual, as if waiting for someone to appear. June's humidity hung like heavy drops in the air, fat oozing insects, hovering.

On this particular morning, his wife had come out to the veranda early with hot coffee, which Parameswaran took gratefully from her and drank. A little later she brought breakfast, crisp brown vadais and steaming soft idlis on a plate with little containers for coconut chutney and sambar. Parameswaran was disapproving, because it was late.

Be quiet, she said, You know how long it takes to make all this.

But Parameswaran, who had spent his entire life working with the government to make the simplest things irretrievably complex, did not believe in the complications of his wife's cuisine. Food required two principles, he considered, that it taste the same always, and that it appear on time. It went without saying that it appear without prompting and that the female portion of the household was responsible for its appearing.

His wife then tried to send him to the market. It was the season for bottlegourd, she said, and if he wanted her special bottlegourd and split pea dish, he'd have to go and get some. But Parameswaran informed her he was not a marketing man; he stretched his legs out into the patch of sun falling through the coconut palms in the front yard and let them burn a little.

By this time, as Parameswaran's wife had noticed, the sun had started to steal into the open veranda and bake the grainy stone at Parameswaran's feet. The bright orange tongues of the canna lilies by the garden wall were drooping a little. Parameswaran sat still and looked over the wall at the street. The salt vendor passed by, pushing his cart piled high with rock salt, coarse crystals of muddy brown and white. The woman selling greens teetered past, basket on her head, calling out the names of her wares. Her eye met his briefly, right in the middle of a full-lunged *Mana-thak-ali!* but Parameswaran did not flinch. Days of sitting still had immured him. The woman looked hard at him as she went by.

Sounds of vessels being washed, clatter of stainless steel and the splash and pouring of water told him the servant-girl was busy doing the day's dishes. The smell of cooking vegetables began to reach him soon, sharp scent of curry leaves and frying mustard and onion and the green smell of beans wrapped in the rich delicate flavor of coconut roasting. Parameswaran shifted slightly in his seat when a crow flew close to the veranda and sat on a branch of the gooseberry tree leaning into the house from the garden. Parameswaran took note of its beady-eyed unfriendly countenance. This was always a sign that someone was coming to visit that day. After a while however, the crow began cawing obnoxiously—twice a premonition—and Parameswaran leapt at it, shooing it away.

At mid-day his wife came out of the house and showed him her index finger which was bleeding. Look, she said, it happened while I was cutting the chilies.

Parameswaran said nothing. The heat had seeped into his armpits and he had taken to walking up and down the small veranda, fanning himself with the newspaper.

Is lunch ready? he asked, apropos of nothing.

Parameswaran's wife regarded him in silence. This she had found had never achieved much in the past but she was bound by custom. Parameswaran kept walking, up and down, up and down. She stood there for a little while, looking.

Perhaps you would like to go outside altogether, she suggested, and turn into straw while you sit in the sun in the garden?

She went away soon after that because Parameswaran would not look at her.

A little after that, Parameswaran who had fallen asleep in his arm-chair woke to an unsettling silence. He looked outside and saw it was past noon; the shadows of the bushes and the palm leaves and the gooseberry stems on the walls had turned around themselves and were slowly lengthening. The heat was a liquid scald on his skin; beads of sweat sat on his pores like wet stones, and his thin cotton shirt and dhoti clung damply to his limbs. What had happened to his lunch?

Saraswathi! he called.

His wife did not appear and Parameswaran was forced to interrupt his useless vigil on the veranda and go inside.

There was food on the table, in the covered stainless steel dishes they used every day. Rice, sambar, and beans that were still warm, vessel sweating a little. Red Andhra mango pickle. A simple meal. Parameswaran sat down at the table and ate his food. His wife did not appear while he was eating. Parameswaran wondered if she was sleeping.

When he was finished he filled a tall glass with water and returned to the veranda.

It was not the first time this had happened, he thought darkly to himself. Lately his wife had taken to being recalcitrant. There were some days she would not come when she was called. And others when she left the house without saying a word to him, visiting old relatives of hers whom he himself had no intention of seeing. Once he had come upon her in the white puja room staring at an agar-bathi as if it were someone's palm she was reading. Running her fingers over the pressed tobacco-dark incense on the stick, looking so intensely at it she didn't hear him at first when he exclaimed sharply at the sight.

Was it age, Parameswaran wanted to know, was it suffering?

But *he* was the one who had suffered. Forty-two years in the government had put odd circles and pouches of flesh under his eyes. Lines of dim rage around his mouth. Saraswathi had never worked, not a day in her life. Out of high school into marriage. What a life, Parameswaran thought. No contact with the ghastly public. The creatures he'd put up with at the office!

A slow hot wind blew into the garden. Scraps of bougainvillea shuddered in it like bits of red paper at his feet. Parameswaran pondered for a moment, fondly, the realization that this, his critical observing of the world, had become quite a ritual. He sat on the veranda and watched as he thought the world because he wanted to be both inside and outside of it. After long, padded years of effacement, by himself and the world, he was, in a languid kind of way, intent on savoring his existence. He read the trouble-ridden newspaper, smoked his unhealthy high-tar cigarettes, walked to the corner store near the clustering huts of the slum-dwellers and the hardware store and the stationery store and the rickshaw-pullers and the taxi-drivers who loitered near the tea-shop with its peeling striped awning and incessant smell of hot milky tea, and bought cigarettes, held forth in a superior tone on the weather and the foibles of the government to whoever was listening and not listening, went to the market to pick out red bulging tomatoes and green spindly *vendaka* if he felt like it. It was like inhabiting a dream, you existed, and the rich, restless shimmering of the dream moved you along, moved you along, you sat still and the whole world occurred inside you. On festival days—Deepavali, Krishna Jayanthi, Pongal—the children came to visit, grandchildren piled up on his lap, the house shrill with talking and food. It was a satisfying life, Parameswaran reasoned. His wife should be grateful.

Four o'clock came soon enough since Parameswaran had eaten so late in the afternoon. Time for tea, steaming and sweet, a household custom. In the street, children were coming home from school, shouting as they went by. The neighbor's wife had returned from her schoolteacher's job at the Corporation school and was screaming at her children.

Parameswaran regarded her with disapproval as she came bustling into the compound of her apartment building, her black wadded bun jiggling on top of her pulled-back gray hair, with that air she had of self-importance. She reminded him of some of the older secretaries in his office. Full of notions and opinions, telling him and every male down the street for half a mile what to think, as if she were the one with the mind and they were all uniformly delinquent.

The heat was beginning to abate a little. Parameswaran's skin had stopped sweating in such abandon and settled into a state of quiet steaming.

Then the sky began to turn, losing its brilliant afternoon blue to a pale sucked-in eggshell. Soon the light would dim and pulse in varying hues of rose, and scraps of cirrus high overhead would drift to scarlet. Parameswaran watched the sky in the evening as he talked, squinting through the gooseberry leaves and the spears of Ashoka rising impossibly into the coconut palms from across the street, and this was his time of day to talk. Saraswathi would sit on the steps cleaning rice or vegetables, listening.

But the sun was setting. People had returned from work. People were taking their evening strolls. Saraswathi did not appear.

When night fell and the smell of jasmine from the garden began slowly to seep into the veranda, sharp and fresh, the smell of steepled buds opening, Parameswaran was compelled to think of things Saraswathi had said to him. In the absence of her voice, her voice began to echo inside him. *Why won't you listen to me* and *when can I do what I want* floated angrily up to him in the thin moonlight. It was to say the least a little eerie and Parameswaran tried to shake off the odd feeling by shuddering abruptly and closing his eyes tight against the world.

But I have to do something with my life pursued him passionately. It was an old echo and particularly irksome. Parameswaran had first heard it in his twenties when Saraswathi had borne two children and was resisting carrying another. Now it was easily followed by *you don't know how difficult this is* and *you are taking my life from me.* That was when she had her fourth child and fell into such a black ennui her mother-in-law had to be recruited to take care of the infants. Later it was silence the house received from her, silence so thick the children grew up in it, a liquid sea of silence that gave to them all their ensuing assumptions about the world. It was not till they had grown, married and left, that the voice had returned, this time thick with sarcasm, with greater fervor, more abandon.

Parameswaran felt sometimes that he lived on the precipice of a bottomless depth, a depth from which his wife's querulous mouth gnawed and chewed at him, and there was always the danger he had to guard against of falling into that engulfing pit and being devoured by her. *You are a selfish, foolish man!* Parameswaran winced. *You make your big noises at home yet you cannot stand up for yourself in the office!* Painful then, and it cut into Parameswaran now like a thin sharp edge of something metallic and sinister, a high whining edge that would not stop until it was replaced by *why can't you do something with your time* and *what do you do sitting all day on the veranda?* And in between, the threats: *I have children I can turn to*, not to mention *I have aunts* (yes, and falling into even greater dilapidation of mind than she was, quite above themselves in the visions of their importance) and *one day you will be sorry.*

Sorry in a scream. *Sorry, sorry, sorry!* Parameswaran thought he heard her voice, her real voice, right there at his elbow and he opened his eyes a fraction and peered at the night and the thick humid air, it was the sound of the crickets in the dark tuning up for their evening cacophonies, shrieking in his ear.

Parameswaran sat there in the rabid moonlight and considered his next action. After all, there were things he could do. Rooms to look into, latches on the back door to examine, a whole terrace to search. The moon was a small carved miniature of itself and it seemed to be pouring its viscous dilutions of light into the blank garden in a particularly insensitive manner, rocking its lucid tongues about his ankles and wrists, mocking him. The bougainvillea and the gooseberry tree had acquired unworldly shadows that leapt and fidgeted about him.

Parameswaran closed his eyes quickly, wanting refuge.

It was too much to consider, he thought. The short crooked whine of crickets in his ear mingled with the voices from the depth, echoing. It was too close, Parameswaran thought, the whole world was too close to him. He wanted to get outside of it, outside. He struggled, *why was it always such a struggle*, such a desire for escape, such a holding back, he wanted to escape, escape—yet why must he always want to escape! He was just an observer, a watcher of things, a man on the veranda, a man on the veranda of the world, the stupid, plunging world, watching it happen. After all he wanted no part in it, none whatsoever, he was outside, he would upset nothing, all he asked for was to sit, watching, sit there quietly, just himself, small self curled up like a mango seed in an armchair, one eye slowly opening, slowly closing, watching the clattering world.

Night came into the house like a serpent, uncoiling itself, and the cool wind entered the small spaces between his toes. The crickets emerged as well and all the little night insects came out, wandering about, entering the house in the moonlight, curious and spirited, settling in shivering trails on his skin.

Temporary Lives

In memory, for my grandmother, Pushpam

One day my husband will die, and before he dies he will hand me a letter with my name scrawled all over it, *Rose Ammal, Rose Ammal*, like a poem, and it will say: forgive me, there is nothing else to ask, I must request this one Christian kindness before I leave. I will gaze out the hospital window into the shell-pink morning and not say a word. The silence will tick like eternity between us, for we are alone in this moment. Victoria, who took the Muslim name Mumtaz Mahal, to please him, is long run off to England. Later I will fold the letter and slide it inside my gold tissue-silk wedding saree. At the funeral service that evening I will wonder what the Buddha advises about this word, *forgive*.

But I am getting ahead of myself. This story begins before 1921, when I was married, or 1905, when I was born, in the village called Idiayangudi in the district the British called Tinnevelly—which we knew in Tamil as Thirunelveli—in the southern part of India. This story begins with my grandfather, our first Christian, an 1862 missionary-convert, who was the wealthiest palmyra farmer in the village, the first in his family to secure a plot of land to call his own, and who had been a palmyra climber for years before that, on other people's plantations. For twenty years of his life, from the time he was ten, he struggled as a common laborer. But with his brothers he hoarded his money, and with his brothers he bought and cleared and sowed the small red patch of soil he could afford. Because the palmyra is a desert tree and will grow anywhere, he was saved. He hired other climbers to climb his trees, he sold pad-hini, nungu, toddy, jaggery—all the many fruits of the palm, all over Thirunelveli district. He sent these off by train to the north, to Madras and Calcutta. He gained a reputation among the British as the best-quality jaggery merchant in Madras Presidency. The whole family of brothers worked at it, yet my grandfather was the one who believed in it enough to make it happen. For years, while I was growing up, my sisters and I would hear this story. Your grandfather had to climb many trees, my father would say, before he could pay a man to climb a tree for him. When you are young, it is natural to have to struggle. *To reach your true-life, you must battle hardship.*

This is why my mother's silence, all through the years of my grow-ing-up, became to me natural, because I believed there were places in the world you had to pass before you reached your *true-life*. Tun-nels deep in the earth's heart, or wide open fields filled with blow-ing wind and rock. Tests of courage meant to be painful, dark. I used to think these places were stones across the water to your real world. *Before you arrived, you had to travel.*

My mother's silence, I learned many years later, began in the year that I was born, 1905, when she fell into a long darkness of the spirit she never fully recovered from. I was her fifth child, and the fifth girl. My mother was frail and small-made, not strong, and she could not bear the thought of having to bear yet another child. But a woman is not whole without a son. She is not far from being bar-ren, the people in the village said, looking at the five of us. Five girls is a curse, not a blessing.

My mother had two more children after me, over a period of six years, and they were both boys. She saved herself in this way from the villagers' contempt. She also restored to good standing the reputation of my father, who was the village schoolmaster. A man, after all, who fathered sons, was more than a man who fathered only daughters. More virile, more a man.

In those years, though, before my brothers were born, all five of us girls experienced my mother's unhappiness, it was a cloud that hung over all of us. My eldest sisters Champa and Malli told me that after the birth she would lie in her room with the windows closed, night and day, and refuse to wake. My sisters took care of me as a baby, because she would not listen when I cried, she simply refused to hear. Even I noticed, very young, when I entered the room, how she would turn away, or find something for me to do somewhere else. Against my will, I began to understand I was a terrible reminder to her, living proof of her inability to conceive a son. I felt, very early, that turning in her, it was inside her, like a seed is inside a fruit, already there. After I felt it, and saw how solid it was, how undeniable, I did not go toward her anymore. I did not ask for her attention. I did not stand in the doorway of her room and look longingly across to her. I understood how it was. I felt what she wanted me to do, and I did it, partly for her, and partly for myself, *I turned too*, I turned away from her.

My two eldest sisters, especially, were saddened by this. They were kind always. I grew up thinking of them in the way, I think, other children think of their mothers. In the night when I woke and called out to them, they answered.

There was always, in my dream, too, the ocean of the *true-life* waiting just beyond the line of jagged rock that scarred my present shore. For now I could only see it hovering in the distance as if from a train-window—shimmer of blue and silver, a beckoning. But I knew I would come some day to water's edge, break past the rocks, the churning, and there I would be, knee-deep in aquamarine, so clear the sand at the bottom glittered, and the pearly shells of crabs and snails glowed like buried gems, rubies or amber. I would look up and the world would stretch before me, all ocean, my own: *breath of my breath, skin of my skin, the world mine.*

I held this dream for so long, consciously and asleep, that it wove its way insidiously into who I was and all through my life sustained me, like water rests on your skin when you bathe and slowly enters and softens. I was not prepared for any other kind of thinking. But one day my dream of the ocean broke, and there was nothing beyond any more, nothing in front of my feet but dark, nothing in the train window but my own reflection, no eyes meeting mine but my own.

When I was sixteen, my mother came to me in the courtyard where I sat hulling the rice, picking out stones and husk and bits of ulundu that had got mixed up in it at the store, and said I was to be married. I looked up at her. Her shadow blocked the sun. The skin around her eyes looked tired. She had been sweeping the compound in front of the house, and there was sweat on her face and neck. She wiped at it with her pallu as she spoke.

It is a good family, she said, We know them well. Not directly, but through our people. We hear only good things about them.

She waited. I didn't know what I was supposed to say. I kept silent.

The family lives in Madras, she said. The boy is a clerk for the government. He just recently got the job—and you know, that is quite prestigious. To work as a clerk for the British government is not a small thing—not everyone can get such a job.

I tapped the morram in my hands, thumb against edge, so the rice leapt and settled, husk flying clean.

The father is a doctor. There are other sons, other children in the house.

I tapped away, my head down, her shadow on the grains in my hands. I could not tell what I felt. I could see the shadow on the rice, the dark slope, white gleaming.

We have fixed the date for the twenty-seventh of May, said my mother. We knew right away it is the kind of family you cannot refuse—we have given them your consent.

I ran my fingers through the rice, and the pale dust from their skins shivered lightly over mine.

They'll treat you well, said my mother. The boy has seen your picture, and he has said he likes you.

She stood a few moments longer beside me. She had said more to me than she usually did. I could not tell what I felt more confused by—what she had said, or the fact of her speaking. The silence in which we lived returned, at the end. It was reassuring—I was used to it. It was almost noon. The heat was in my bones. I could feel the sweat in the crease behind my knees slip down my calf, under my half-saree. There were crows in the coconut trees, hoarsely calling. Parrots screeched. I sat very still, my fingers idly touching the rice. She stood quietly beside me. Then she went inside.

Red earth, palmyra, huge blooms of cacti. I saw these from the train as we sped north to Madras.

I was afraid, but I was also full of secret excitement. I wondered if the ocean of my true-life was at last going to approach. I tried to imagine how it might look, far off in the distance, a glisten of blue and silver, a beckoning.

Steel tracks stretched before me. Steel tracks in an arid landscape. I sat so still, and looked so hard, that the *clack-clack* of the wheels on the tracks began to beat in synchrony with the *pulse-in-pulse-out* of my heart, and the sky, packed with fish-scale clouds, came thundering toward me. I felt after a while I was the train itself, sealed within its cabins of steel, bound to its ancient tracks, with its many windows the eyes of my soul unleashed on the still, unmoving world as it hurtled onward. Every now and then I saw long rice fields, so green the water and spring shoots in them shimmered iridescent, like parrot-wings, on the land. I was hungry, I took hope from these.

At the time of the wedding, I had only glimpses of the man I would marry. When we were exchanging vows, at the part where you had to say *until death do us part*, my new husband swiveled his head around to give me a penetrating stare, and I, discomposed, unsure of the right thing to do, glanced up and caught its spectacled scrutiny. It felt cold, passionless, his gaze. I could not tell what he was thinking. It felt like he was trying to read my mind, or wrest something from me. I looked away.

We went to the studio in town the day after we got married. I had to wear my wedding saree again. I sat on a high-backed, ornately carved armchair made of teakwood in the studio. The cushion beneath me was scarlet and made of velvet. The armrests too velvet. I looked down, I did not lean my arms on them. I clasped my fingers in my lap for the picture. I did not look up until the photographer asked me to.

Gold rode high on my arms. I could feel the smooth cool weight of gold hanging from my earlobes and resting on the bare skin of my neck. The band of gold around my midriff kept my saree and veil and pallu in place and leaned tight into my breath.

My veil was tulle. The cloth was imported from England, and it was very light, and fluffy and full about my shoulders. My mother had pinned it back to my hair, all wound up into a plait piled on the nape of my neck. There was white baby powder on my face.

My husband stood beside me in full British splendor—a suit with a waistcoat and chain, no less. We had not said much to each other. He said, Careful! when we came out of the church into white sunlight and I almost tripped on the steps. I said, I can't see my parents, can you see them, when we arrived at the school hall for the reception afterward.

At the studio, with the bright lights focused blindingly on us, he turned to me and gave me a white cotton man's handkerchief. Here, wipe your face, he said. You're sweating.

He seemed very young. He wore his hair parted in the center and slicked back with oil. His moustache was small, trimmed very carefully at the ends. His hands were delicately shaped, almost like a woman's. The fingers were long and thin. The nail-faces oval. I thought, this is a man who cares about himself.

Three nights after the wedding, my husband consummated our vows, despite my confusion. I had never known the touch of a man on my body. I had not expected the physical pain I felt. But I found out soon enough it was only the beginning. Through the first ten years of our marriage, I learned what my mother knew, I learned the living of a woman's life. I opened a book I had not known existed, I turned the pages: *the meeting of bodies, woman-blood, man-semen, the flaring open, distending of the hidden womb, forming of child-*

*hands, child-eyes, in the supine darkness, the long tear and pull and
in-held breath, pulsing of the universe, the final freeing, woman-body
expelling flesh: child-heart, child-soul.*

I bore nine children, seven of whom lived—five of these sons.
Like my mother, I learned silence. All things seemed to take place
in silence. A woman's world, I learned, was shaped and formed of
silence, its contours (*husks falling from rice*) were silence, its breath
(*rice ground to a powder*) silence, its flesh and bone (*milk heaving
in its skin of cream as it boiled*) silence. The sounds I heard were
silence. I gave to my children the yellow spill of my breast's flowing
milk, and silence.

I lived without knowing I lived, in the echo of other women's
voices, in the sleep of other women's dreams. My feet were held
within the jeweled slippers of all the women who had come this
way before, I heard their anklets ringing when I walked, felt their
birth-pains when I heaved. Knowing and not knowing, I fit my soles
in the footprints of all the women who had walked before me.

For many years, I dreamt repeatedly of newborns, their bare
heads round and shiny with birth-fluid, eyes scrunched tight,
voices raised in rage at the pain of birth. Sometimes they tumbled
in a stream in the middle of the house, clawing and scratching at
each other. Sometimes they were miniscule, thumb's width, fin-
ger-thick, they pushed up against my face, my hair, my clothes,
pulling, pushing, tearing. Sometimes they floated, man-size from
the ceiling, the walls, they hung upside-down in space, eyes greedy
and vengeful, they looked grotesquely down at me.

I was never present in these dreams as a figure or face or silhouette that could be seen. The babies crowded, demanded visibility.
I was hidden in this crowding, shrouded by limbs, buried by eyes.
Each time I woke I felt the residue of that crowding and I felt I
knew, even then, I myself, thanks to the screaming children torn
from me, I would never be seen.

Where was the dream of the true-life in those years? Was there a
dream? Was there a scent of the possible in my wakings, my tend-

ings, my sleep? A longing I kept sealed in my heart like an envelope to be opened on another shore?

I do not know.

The wind passes. At night you hear it in the trees high above the house, it goes through the knife-blades of the coconut trees, palm upon palm, like a melody.

The rain passes. It comes from the Indian Ocean—a handful of clouds, a scattering—and goes toward the Ghats, pausing for a moment on the shore that is our town.

When my last child was seven years old, my mother died. I took the train with three of the children, Rani, Stephen, and the youngest, Martha, and went to the Idaiyangudi house for the funeral. My father was very old, and greeted me on the veranda. I have done your mother a great disservice, he said. I used up her life. He did not have to explain to me what he meant. My sisters and brothers were all in the house. We tried to reassure him, but secretly, in our hearts, as we sat with her body for the night, and kept the candles lit, we felt we understood. No one said it, but in our minds we could all see a room closed in daytime, all the windows closed, and my mother forever asleep on the bed, her back turned to us.

I returned to the day to day routine of cooking, washing, feeding the children. The house grew around me like a living thing. The walls crept, the doors crept, the rooms leafed and tendriled around me like a dusty vine. Hands reached out to me from the peeling plaster. Limbs locked with mine on the terrace.

I lived like a snail deep in its living shell, unable to move too far from its silvery shelter. I learned the shape and texture of the walls with my hands, the peeling of rust on the veranda's trellis-work. I listened to the bright light from the high windows speak in planes to the floor, I communed with corners where dust slept. I listened to sparrows, to the crackle of wood burning in the kitchen.

Small things came toward me, their hands open: rain in the papaya, the deep mysterious hearts of flowers, the white pigeons on the neighbor's roof. I took small things into my hands.

I came to know that who I was equaled *who the woman in the next house was, and the next and the next, all the way down to the end of the street.* We lived the same lives. It didn't matter what we were—Hindu or Muslim or Christian. We woke to the calling of our children, to the long day of cooking and cleaning and listening, pallu over our heads in the heat, saying little, listening. When my husband spoke, I listened. When my mother-in-law spoke, I listened. When my father-in-law, my sisters-in-law, my brothers-in-law spoke, I listened. When my children spoke, I listened.

Those who heard me speak were women or children: the woman who sold keerai every morning at eleven in our neighborhood, the woman who came to work in our house, the women who came to see my father-in-law, the *doctor-sir,* my own children.

Time slipped through my fingers like rice when you clean it

One day I woke, my sons were grown, my daughters ready to be married. In five shapes, my sons grew into their father. I was their mother, the woman who brought them forth into the world. I was a woman. When my sons spoke, I listened.

All through those years, in my mind, I was seated at a train window, travelling. I was looking across a loneliness of desert to a distant ocean.

The ocean was often invisible, so thinly silver a line it vanished in the sky's shining.

But as the years went by, I dreamt the ocean grew sharper in color as you approached, tangibly blue, green, violet. I dreamt it roared and sprayed on the rocks like a wild and buoyant spirit at play. I dreamt the sound and spray of it. In the midst of all the water once I dreamt a singing—at once of the earth and unruly, out of this world, a vibrance, soul-passion issued on the vigor and power of a human voice—*my voice.*

It was this, hearing the singing in my dream, that made me realize my own long-grown, long-coffined desire for a voice, a way to release all the depths of mingled feeling in my heart, buried and tombed in silence. I wanted to break the silence with my words. With my own voice, break it open.

Being a woman, doing a woman's work, was the darkest tunnel, I thought, in the world. I believed in ends and beginnings then. I believed I could pass through it.

But then the change in our lives that would continue until my husband died began. One afternoon he said to me: you are not educated after all.

It is true, I had stopped studying after the tenth standard.

We were sitting outside in the front garden. He was talking about his work, how it was so different with the new government (it was 1951) after the British left. He had made his way up the ranks over the years and he had a fine position now, as Secretary with the Ministry of Education.

He was much respected. At church, he was always on the board of some committee or the other. He had a great presence in church, he stood for something. The pastor often brought visiting Bishops and senior members of the Diocese around after the service to meet my husband. And at home, there were always people coming to see him, to ask his advice, or bring him something—a box of sweets, a crate of fruit—for some favour done. It was much like when his father was alive, and patients came in to see the old man or bring gifts. I did not get a chance usually to sit and talk with him.

But then he rarely spoke to me. He said little to the women as a rule. He spoke to our sons, to his brothers, to other men. I had learned very young this is how it was, men spoke this way. Women were not for the speaking to.

But this evening he said his work was getting more and more difficult, the old system was better, these people were out to dishonor you all the time, and I said, when he was finished, this is what I said: you mustn't be discouraged, I am sure no one can deny the quality of your work and your experience.

He said then it was clear he could not talk to me. That I could not follow the nuances of his tribulations. He said, even Victoria can follow me when I speak.

I said, who is Victoria?

He looked exasperated. She is the daughter of my friend, Victor, he said, the one who is in medical college. He started to smile as he said this, at the thought of how bright she was.

I said, I would have become a doctor if my father had let me.

He snorted at that and fell into silence. He didn't talk to me about his work after that.

That was the first time I heard him speak of Victoria.

Her name floated around the house like the scent of cinnamon after that—deep, accented, ambiguous. My children spoke of her. They looked at me and away, they stopped talking when I entered rooms.

So, very early on, I knew there was something there, something I felt in my bones I did not want to know.

I was reading a lot on my own then, rocked from the world into caverns of my own self, filled with searching.

At first only the Christian publications that lay around the house—my *Daily Bread*, a life story of Sadhu Sundar Singh. Then I found some of my children's textbooks and I began to read them— *Ancient Indian History*, the *History of Religions*, a book on Hindu Scripture, a book on Buddhist thinking, poems by Rabindranath Tagore, translated into English.

I looked long at a picture postcard of the seated Kamakura Buddha a cousin-sister had sent us a long time ago from her missionary travels in Japan and China. Closed eyes, crossed legs, the body lotus'd, folded and flowering in repose. The drape and Grecian fold of stone on the statue falling as if in solemn, natural curves around the in-held heart of the tranced, unawoken god.

I knew from the beginning that something in Buddhism was calling to me. The peace and sanctuary of the Buddha's closed eyes spoke to all the soreness of my seeing. I wanted that inwardness. Here, in this life, this moment. Not after my death, in heaven, as the resurrected Christ promised. But in this living.

Then I came across a passage from one of the great Buddhist masters that iterated the Buddhist credo: that our deaths were knit into our lives, that we were born, already broken. That to live as the

Zen Buddhists did, in the here and now, the only moment, was the only true living.

Something opened inside me like a red wound, a flower when I read those words.

A very strange thing. I could no longer believe only in the Christian idea of salvation, the karmic afterlife in which recognition was conferred, and heaven and hell, both terrible and all-consuming approached us as reward or sentence, one or the other. I found I did not want the God of my childhood, the God of my husband. I could feel how I was turning from Christ, deep inside, a deliberate turning. I did not question it.

Yet I kept going to church all this time. Because there is always the life of the surface to be lived, and I excelled at it.

I also knew by now something large was happening in my husband's life. He was away from home for weeks. He was short-tempered, impatient, when he returned. The amount of money he gave me for the house was dwindling.

My older children worked and gave me money for the house and the family. Much was done in silence. I said little to them. But they must have talked among themselves. They respected my need, unspoken, for silence. They gave me money, I used it. There was rice to be bought, and parripu, and meat, fish, vegetables. There was the electricity bill to pay, curtains to be sewn, clothes for school and work to be bought. We ran the house as before, we tried to keep up the same standards.

Then of course, the moment arrived, the moment that all things ended in my seeing, all things broke, and the ocean of my dreams disappeared forever.

I was prepared, and I was not prepared.

I knew it was going to happen, yet I could not have foretold the depth and intensity of my own reaction.

My husband came to me one morning, after yet another long interlude in the south, where he said he had had work to do—and he said, without preface, he had become a Muslim, he had changed his name, and he had married another woman. He said, as a Muslim, a man can have up to four wives—and this is why I have done this. He said: I want you to know you are the mother of all my children. I would not harm you in any way. He said, your position will not change in any way. Your life will be the same. Only mine will change. I will live half the year in Vellore with Victoria, where she has a medical practice.

He said, in my heart I will always be a Christian.

It was mid-morning; the day's heat was in the room. On the table was a glass of cold water I had just drawn from the clay pot for him.

At the fore of my thoughts was a chaotic, irrelevant questioning: what did it mean that we were exchanging gods so easily, that we had both come to this, professing one God on the outside and pursuing another within?

Outside, on the mango tree, there were crows. I heard them calling. My husband was fifty-four years old. I was forty-nine. I looked down at the tumbler of water and in its still, circular surface, I saw my own questioning.

I went to the beach that evening. No one came with me. My children may have thought I was going to church. I did not correct this impression.

I walked down the long stretch of still-hot six o'clock sand, taking my slippers off, sinking barefoot in the debris from shells, nets, and fish-scales that litter the Marina, toes scrunching in and out of white sand. People crowding the sand.

By water's edge on damp sand I walked, waves cool and foamy on my ankles, drenching the cotton of my saree. I did not lift the pleats up with one hand. I let the waves buffet, flow over me, I went in deeper and deeper.

Children were playing beside me. Fisher children, bare-chested, diving and swimming and shouting and tossing water at each other. A man with a child on his shoulders stood to my left. His wife beside him, her saree neatly hitched up at her waist. Jasmine in her hair.

The waves blew sand and shell at me. They were coming in higher now, up above my waist. My hands wet, legs wet, saree wet, face drenched in spray.

The man with the child called to me above the sound of the wind. *Madam, Madam! What are you doing, the tide is coming in—you're going in too far!*

The ocean was a deep, heaving green. The sky grey. No hint of aquamarine anywhere.

I looked down. I could not see my feet in the sand when the waves swirled and the sand swirled and ropes of seaweed, dead chrysanthemum tossed into the sea from a funeral wreath perhaps, caught and clung.

Madam, come back!

This was my life, I realized. It was not waiting in the distance, clear glass, lit and ringing. It had never waited. It was here. It had always been here. And it was not mine, not my own secret to break open and into—it was vast, it was endless, it was full of debris, and I was knee-deep in it.

Madam! Amma!

I looked down, and I could no longer see the ocean.

The water was black around me. The water was dead.

The water was an emptiness, a black chasm, I fell through it. I closed my eyes, I could feel myself falling. Born, already broken, I thought. Our lives broken inside us. Our lives a breaking.

And what is the life after?

After the man on the beach had saved me, literally dragged me out of the water and thrust me, dripping, dazed, on the sand, people gathering around me, round-eyed, scolding me for my thoughtlessnes, I sat, saree a cold second skin around me, looking at the sea.

What was to come? What was the life after to be like?

The dream of the true-life was dead in me then. I knew there was to be no true-life shimmering in the future. There was one-life, there had been one life all along. And right now it was dead water foaming around me. Ropes of sea weed around the neck, closed eyes of fish, ground and eaten shell. It was death, a constant dying.

Not the life I wanted.

The sea heaved and crested and foamed ahead, steadily darkening. Wind blew. Salt crusting on my skin as it dried.

I wondered what my husband had changed his name to. I wondered how Victoria was newly named, she too had become a Muslim.

I had thought that the lives I had lived were makeshift lives, in-between lives. Before-lives, in-waiting for the true life. But here was the ocean, here was the true-life, here, where it had been, all along, here, where it would never recede from. Never dreamed-of, unwanted.

A streak of lightning broke through the sky. Its white shimmering falling on the water like a heavenly shining. I looked at the explosive gleam of silver water and saw the high, uneasy churning. A ragged wind blew sand into my face. It was going to rain. All around me, people were leaving. Down the long row of vendors selling hot groundnuts and sundal, the yellow flicker of kerosene lamps shook in the wind.

I picked myself up, took my slippers in my hand and began to walk up the beach. Every now and then a white shell glittered in the sand. I bent without thinking, picked it up. I shook the sand off, held it in my hand. I smoothed its blunt, eroded contours, I felt the satin inside the mouth. Then I picked another, and another, and another. Some of these shells were broken. They were bits of shell—a curve, a flattened scoop, some shiny, ended part of a once living mollusk. I picked them all up. I felt I would never have the true-life of my dreaming. But perhaps I could actually live in the in-between, one makeshift to another, keeping that before me, the transience. All my dreaming broken. All my lives temporary.

My children were careful in what they said to me afterward. I saw them watching me now and then, as if worried, as if uncertain. They were afraid to speak. They did not speak. Silence, the river of seeming calm between us, resumed its usual flow.

My husband lived with us a few weeks or so at a time. He would go away and come back after a month. My daughters-in-law began to take over the duties of the house. They made time for me to rest, supervised the servants who helped cook and clean for us, called me in to eat.

There was no one among all our relatives who did not know what had happened. I wondered what they thought sometimes. I would walk into rooms and voices would drop, eyes turn away. Sometimes I felt a tide of sympathy sweep over me from some quarter. Yet I knew I could not rest on it. Because I was a woman, and a woman carries her husband's name with her.

I thought then: *In the house of my marriage there are many rooms. Who built this house? Not me, nor my husband. My husband opens the door and steps out into the world. The sun removes itself. The walls grow and grow around me. The windows seal themselves. Vines and roots wrap themselves round the brick, the glass, the wood. I wander from room to room, hearing the sound of my breath. I look through the dust-grimed, vine-wrapped windows at the world.*

When I walk in the streets with my children I carry the house around me like a cloak. If I stepped outside it, let myself be seen in public without that concrete burkah, I would be a woman exposed and naked, revealing her family's shame to the world.

There were some things, I learned, a woman could do. After church, one Sunday morning, I made breakfast for the beggars who came knocking on our gate. That is how it started. Word passed around. More and more people came by from the slums on Sunday mornings. I had my son bring in long wooden benches from a school nearby. I put them in the backyard. Every Sunday our household fed the poor.

My husband did not say a word. He seemed distantly approving. He approved my *piety.*

My children began to regard me in a somewhat exalted light, as if I were a saint. This was such a Christian thing to do.

I also went to church in the evening for the six pm Service, even if I'd gone once already in the morning with the family. The hand-rickshaw man on our street came to the door regularly at five-thirty every Sunday evening. I closed the gate behind me, climbed in, he unfurled the big fanned shade over my head. It was a restful moment.

My children did not know I had stopped praying or reading the

Bible. Somewhere inside I had slammed doors shut against the old Christ I had known, the God of the Bible, my God. I kept the postcard with the Buddha on it in my bible—I took it out and looked at it often.

The house of my marriage still grew around me its walls of brick and ivy, but I knew now my soul was not inside it.

I went to church to be alone, to sit with the organ's slow sound before Service, white flowers at the altar, dark pews, dusk turning to violet in the sky, the slowly-turned-on lights of the crystal chandelier. I went to sing.

Our church had a large compound around it, and on one side of it, at the far end, a graveyard. On the other side, beyond a small garden, was the pastor's house. You could look out of the big double-doors of the church on either side and see: flowers, sky, trees, headstones. In the evenings there were birds in the shoeflower bushes and the gulmohar and the tamarind—sparrows, mynahs, parrots, pigeons.

It was the old people's service. You looked around and you saw all the old people in the parish, the ones who couldn't make it at seven for the Morning Service.

I lifted my voice up to the heavens, I sang. The songs themselves were not uplifting, at least, not the melodies. The songs were old. Old English hymns, written in the seventeenth and eighteenth century. Our organist had a predilection for the most mournful among them. But I liked hearing the sound of my voice, raised in song, against the closely-held leaves of the hymnal.

Victoria and my husband were together for eighteen years. Then she divorced him and married a doctor friend from her college days, they emigrated to England. She was still young, after all, she must have been in her late thirties then. My husband was seventy-two. He came back to the house to live, and he kept to himself and his routines. Between us, there was too much silence to overcome.

The heart and lung trouble he started having in his sixties returned. He was under treatment and faithfully took his medication, yet, within one year, his heart gave out. The day we sat together by the hospital window, and the light, new gold, began to enter the room, it is true I could not speak. But I looked at the letter once more, to please him, and I put my hand over his. Both our hands were warm and trembled. He asked me if I would sing, and I opened the hymn book. I looked for the song Amazing Grace, and I started to sing. Something glistened in his eyes, faintly. His breath was labored. His eyes beginning to close. I kept on singing. I heard the strength in my voice as I raised and lowered it, feeling like a rower in a boat, pushing and forging a way through a wave-filled ocean. His body heaved a sigh. A small whistling sound escaped his lips. I knew he was leaving by the end of the first verse but I could not stop. The minutes passed. The morning came into the room, and I was singing.

Same Blue Sky

◡ I'd never thought the day would come when I would look across the leap I had made, from a crowded little town in the middle of India across continents of land and water to a sprawling suburb in Northern Virginia, and actually think: my life, *it's not that different.* The sky collapses to blue. Day after night after day. Birds wake us, birds put us to sleep. Dusk yawns and stretches. Moon-halves hang in the middle of the street. Some days the same blue sky I knew in India burns high. Sapphire-blue, hot-sea blue. (Copper-sulphate and turquoise-blue, filmy soap-bubble-blue.) And green vein-on-the-skin blue, skin of slaughtered cows, skin of our human, woman lives. Vein and skin and texture of our lives the same here as in our first homes. Tenor, shape, and sound.

I came, six years ago, newly married, my visa signed and stamped, my distress at being removed from my native soil, my no-knowledge about my green-card husband. (Virgin bride: an arranged marriage, a foreign-settled groom.) I came, reluctant. I came: gilted, thali'd, bound for the future. I came, without knowledge.

*

The day knowledge came to me—the all-surpassing, all-compassing knowledge I did not think I would ever come to—I was surprisingly well prepared. I had seen and heard too much. I knew, I already knew. I knew, and did not know, I knew.

I was listening to a bird sing at the time.
A single bird, singing the same song, over and over.
The same.
Same strophe of notes, same flicker of breath, same *repeat and pause, repeat and spill, repeat, repeat* from the bird's repeating throat.

I heard the bird array its notes in wind, over and over, the same handful of notes in wind. I listened without listening until I heard. I told myself it was one song the bird knew, stitched deep into its throat so it had no recourse but to sing it, strewing notes in the same pattern, over and over. I told myself our own songs were sewn into our souls, so deep our hearts beat their rhythm, our blood pounded their beat, our breath echoed theirs. I told myself if I listened hard enough I would hear my singing.

The day is now.
The hour is now.
The whole world devolves into the now: of a bird's song, a moment's breath, a moment's knowledge.

My husband says: *leave me alone!*

There is a moment between the not-knowing and the knowing that is a singular moment. It is luminous, a temporal space riddled through with possibility. It is sheathed deep in the unknowing. It is haloed, ringed and singed alive by the future knowing. It is pregnant with the knowing to come, yet it holds itself wombed, unbreached.

*

The song he sings repeats itself: *I am a man, I will do what I want.*

Neither not-knowing nor knowing. A little of both perhaps. But neither entirely.

*

I folded clothes in this moment. I carried up and down the public apartment stairs the white-weave Walmart plastic baskets of clothes, dirty and clean, colored, white, shirts and pants, skirts, sarees, salwars, bras. Permanent press, delicate (knits), cotton (sturdy), light soil, normal, heavy. I rinsed and spun all day, *warm warm, warm* and *cold, cold cold.* I dried, tumbled, folded.

My husband says: *take care of the child!* Deflecting attention from himself like a carefully-angled mirror. Like a child.

My daughter follows me from room to room. She pulls at my salwar, my muslin chunni. I am the world to her. I am the world and four walls, the walls of the world around her. She plays on the floor, tumbling. She says, Da Da! Where is Da Da going?

Who is the bird? Who is the knot in new-leaf sky, clenching unclenching voice in wind?

Smoke in the air of our common breathing. Incessant smoke. Abrading, coruscating smoke. My husband smokes Marlboros, gritty, unrelenting, yard upon field of smoke. The coils of it linger, the smell of it: in the walls, the brocade curtains, hardwood floors, cotton dhurries on the floor. It plays on the nostrils like a burning, scores and sears the throat. It settles in the lungs like spiky ash, I can feel it when I breathe. And my daughter chokes. She coughs, she reels, she chokes. My husband opens a window and watches her. Smoke and cold air for our breath. Smoke and winter, winter and smoke. Smoke in the clothes I wash, smoke in their drying. Smoke so fine and so bound (thali-bound, bound by its being-

there, horoscope- and palm- and destiny-bound, astrally intended)
it will not leave us.

A single bird extends, becomes a chorus. A choir of birds, a congregation. Each eye on a different page, each throat issuing forth a different song.

*

I looked in the mirror in the moment. I stole the moment into my
seeing, stole my seeing in the moment.

I saw: trouble in the eyes. I saw: the blank map of the face. I saw: the
trundling of trains, the long disappearance of the concrete platform, leaves flickering sun on the tracks. I saw: the journeys of the
past and the future in the map of the present. I saw: the shapes of
things as they had been, the shapes of what was to come. I saw: my
future in that moment, I saw a train of futures, I saw trains heading
to different destinations. I saw: trains pulling out of the moment's
station, big wheels turning. I turned away from the mirror as the
seeing unfolded. I turned away. I did not see inside the trains, I did
not see who was inside them.

You are in a new country, my husband says. You won't know what
to do if you don't do as I say. *You won't know! You won't know! I know
what you won't know!*

How long in a new country to learn what to do? How long for the
country to lose the new? How long the not-knowing? I step into
my street-clothes, pull Plum Ice across my mouth, I blow my cut-
short-to-the-shoulders hair into curls. My husband sweeps his eyes
across my face. Wells of cool and stagnant water, odor of decay in
them: his eyes. He says: tie up your hair. Are you a street-woman?
He says: Where are you going, dressed like that? Or simply: Where
are you going?

*

In other words: what is it that needs to be done I cannot do? Is there a need for your stepping into the world? Is there a need for the world? *I am the world!* I and the world outside—we are the world! No other equation, no other joining! In other words: make this room your world. You want a world? Make the walls your world! Paint a pot for the windowsill, hang a painting on the wall! The walls can be your world—not what lies outside.

It is difficult to listen to the song of the bird and stand still in one room, one apartment, one suburban neighborhood, like an unkempt statue, desirous but limited.

*

I walk to the park everyday with the child. I sit in the park. In the cold. I listen to the birds. I see starlings descend in clouds of crying in the oaks. I see the tear and underseam of wing, the manic brilliance of eyes, the oil-slick rainbow gleam of starling-body in sunlight. I play with the other children, talk to the women—the childsitters, college students, housewives. I walk to the grocery store in a strip mall four blocks from our home. I walk to the hairstylist's, I take the child. I am the DayCarer, NightCarer, Weekend Worker on no pay, no leave. I am the Cook-er, the Sweep-er, the Vacuum-er, the Wash-er of Clothes and Dishes, the quintessential Housewife. I am the Queen of the House Walls and Windows, the Curtains, the Blinds. I swob and dust, Mop and Glow, cook and clean, steam and dry. I dress my daughter up in clothes I sew, and I sew at night with the TV on, I watch sitcoms as I sew.

My husband says: there's no need for you to learn to drive!
   (*There's no-need, no-need, no need need need!*)
   If you need to go somewhere, all you have to do is tell me (*all you have to do to do!*) I will take you! (*I will take you!*) Where do you need to go?

My husband says: there's no need to go to the store on your own!

There's no need to go to the salon! *There's no need, no need!* I will drive! I will take you!

The scattering of the old among the new like grain or salt or sand or rain. The old encroaching into the new—like everlasting ocean, like mold in bread or a woman's womb, old tea staining the white of silk. The old order seeps and stains, builds flakes and peelings of dark on new walls. The old drips through his eyes, his mouth, his eternal hunger for my submissiveness. The old is in his spine, deep within, it holds him, here, upright. The old sustains and buoys him, the old calls and recalls him—he rushes to the old, stands, showering each day in the old, soaped and scrubbed and rinsed in the old; he listens to the songs of his childhood, called, recalled; he holds the old measures of distance with his parents on the phone; he does what the old way demands, he is the good son, the inviolable, irreproachable, the perfect son, he does what he is told; he watches old Hindi films he borrows from the video store, week after week— the same old songs of love and betrayal, the same old reverence for the old; he towels and wraps himself in the old, it is comfort and solace and song to him—he sings in the shower as he bathes; the voice, untuned, he brings to the singing is old, the tunes are old, the songs are old.

Yet my husband believes he is a man of the moment.

He says he lives among the new, the raw, the being-made, the first transformations of intent to data 01 10 11 00: he lives in a cubicle at work, writing strings of code with his computer keys, string after string after string. He says yes to the knot in his tie, yes to the starchy collar at his neck, yes to the shine of his black-cowskin shoes. Yes yes yes! He doesn't see the old among these things. Yes to the new, the being-made, the shiny shoe, slaughtered-cow-shoe, of death! Yes to the trappings of wealth, the steadily American quest for the manicured, the shiny, the polish of all exteriors. Yes to the glitter and rigor and exacting eye of surfaces. Yes to the new that reeks of the old, that is the old dressed up as the new, parading

159

as the new, the never-been-done-before, the time-to-come. Yes to the old marching rampantly ahead through the streets of the present like a Spanish conquistador whose uniform is praised as new, a builder of British empires whose decimations of life are beheld as new, a Catholic colonizer of worlds whose language encroaching into every tongue is heard as new. Yes to the old English austerity of will, the tight upper lip and the cold Teutonic eye, the ancient myth-making of manhood as invulnerable, iron, the masks and the secrecy and the covering-over, the wrapped-suit steel of the phallic drive, the holding of the human flesh, worm-like, twisted and sheathed beneath its shatter-proof vest of the new, the technologically-equipped, the so-called-civilized. Yes to the colonized, the quarried and picked and powdered and carried and ground-up-into-concrete mind, yes to being seen in team-player guise, corralled and shepherded, shaved and creamed, cologned, talc'd, trimmed and gelled—outwardly professional-ized.

My husband keeps his hunger for the old hidden beneath his new-American face.

The face he wears to work in his multi-national, linear-motive firm structured smoothly around the singular God of Profit is what I call a face beside his face, a face he takes up and puts down at will, a business face, a one-mind, one-thought, one-deed face, a roving, shark's-eye, electric-ray-sting, cobra-strike face. This face is soaked in the future. It is packed in the brine of ambition, thinly glazed in the need for a publicly recognizable success. It is a face well-suited to his place in the world, because it is a running face, the face of a man in motion, unable to stand still, keep still, stay still. Like all the faces in his firm, it is a hungry face. It looks for what it can use with an unwavering and mathematical passion. It searches and roves, leaps ahead and springs, turns and returns to a blandness intended to invite you in: *come in, come in! Look at my house of pale and empty cream, my sweetly empty house! Come flying in—spill every secret in this room, tell every tale, look how clear and cool and white these walls are! No one will hear us! No one renounce us! No one betray us!* Till every secret is told, every fact laid bare, every bone turned over. It adds and multiplies, cavorts through differentials, cascades down variables, calculates your assets to the nineteenth decimal, checks and weighs you in its balance books and reduces you to your liabilities, your ineptitudes, your plummeting market-value, your probabilities of failure, your insignificance. It weighs the world in numbers, numbers that fluctuate and swell, that rise and fall, that disappear and return, that square- and cube-root you to your primest essence: *insect, you are pinned. Thorax, diaphragm, chitin, sheath—arms, legs, bulging eyes—there's a name to your holdings now, a laboratory tag, a marker of death. Wriggle as you might, you are forever held in this finite series, this set of integers, branded, counted, buried, bled. Your use is known, your voids plumbed, your uncertainties read.* It is the face with which he meets the business faces of his day, the face with which he greets each face on the street, in the complex where we live, on the train.

It is the face he clings to. As fortress, shield, refuge. As flag and shining beacon of his all-seeing, all-knowing, all-controlling intelligence.

So I knew. I had known for a long time, I knew. I had lived too long with his need.

*

Da Da! Why does Da Da smoke, pacing up and down the window outside Starbucks where a woman alone sits, reading? Who is Da Da looking at? Why must we sit in the car in the parking lot after our trip to the mall and wait for him? Look, Da Da is smoking! Up and down, back and forth, as if it were a colder night than it is, up and down, back and forth! Where is Da Da going?

*

The moment is a bird, it is winged, it is filled with sound—*repeat*

repeat lingering. The moment is a mirror's face, a silver behind the glass, a sharp, unquenchable seeing. The moment approaches, I hear its footsteps, glass on glass, clear and sharp, metal chimes in wind.

I fold the bras of cotton and of silk, the lace panties, the thick Fruit of the Looms my husband wears, the white dress shirts, the finely patterned socks. I fold and pile, fold and pile.

The woman is Indian. Face of my face, skin of my skin, eyes of my eyes, hair of my hair. I look at her and I see myself there in her place. I look at her face and it is mine and not mine—there is a sisterhood between us, a sisterhood of skin and country. She is made as I am of rain and memories, long letters and plane-rides, pickle made from green mangoes bought in a city marketplace and packed in red chilies and mustard oil, aplums and bay leaves, Kerala cardamom and cloves, Nilgiris cinnamon, Assam tea, pink-silk sweetness of badam kheer, sugarcane juice sold fresh with ginger and lemon and crushed ice at roadsides, Bengal cottons, silkworm-death and tourist brilliance of Kanchipuram silks—rain on roofs and new jasmine blooming at night outside a window, coconut-palm moon on the face. She is young, she is alone, she is flyaway thin. She is American to the bone—her blouse is white and low-cut, her jeans are blue and old, her hair is silky, upswept with a butterfly-comb. She is Indian and she is American—both myself and not-myself— she sits, unaware, reading her paper, at this Starbucks window, sipping her café au lait, next to the Barnes and Noble whose books she carries heaped in a pile on the counter.

We walked past the Starbucks on our way to the car. Our eyes met as we passed. I in my blue salwaar-kameez, my new curls, my Payless heels, my child beside me, my long handbag, waiting for my husband to open the passenger door with his only copy of the car keys, jangling in his hand. She smiled. I could not bear to see her face, that smiling face, open face, Indian, knowing face, I steeled myself, I looked away.

She sits and reads while my husband leaves us in the car and returns for a smoke, up and down, back and forth, outside her window.

*

From the third-floor window of our bedroom I see trees budding across the street. Redbud, dogwood, oak—mauve pink white. Some limbs of trees still unleafed. Spring-green in the air—pistil-green, clear calyx-green.

What is it my husband sees in the woman he wants me not to become, to turn toward, to emulate?

What is it he wants from her he wants me not to have, to find for myself, to give?

The same illusion of will. Restoration, through the child-bird's throat in spring: *re-see re-feel repeat.*

I am the virgin, the horoscope bride, the woman led, fore-ordained, by the ancient placement of stars and planets to his side. I am the girl his parents found, his parents believed would make a perfect wife for their son. I am the Indian girl, the home-town girl, the stay-at-home girl, the married-at-twenty girl, the mother at twenty-one. I am the lucky one, the picked, the chosen, from the pool of women hungry to be bound to a green-card man, a tall, a fair, an engineering man. I am the old, the shape and smell and feel of his childhood, his city, his home—the mother he was born to, the sister he played with, the sister he found a husband for. I am the woman who tends him when he is sick and not sick, who makes available for him all the daily food and care and sex in his life. I am the one who makes his potency known by my bulging womb, the toddling child. I am the known, the familiar place—surveyed, mapped and measured, under control. Bangled, thali'd, surma'd, mehendi'd, bindhi'd, salwaar'd, plaited—I am his (sex-sharer, bed-warmer, owned, flagrant possession, public display, mother of his child) *wife*, and so the other-name of his malehood, his *manhood, masculinity*, power, his ability to own.

She is new, the unknown place. Territory unmapped. Indian, she is close to who I am and to who he is—yet she is outside his control. She is free of his belief that as male he necessarily owns what is female in the world. She is a bird, sitting in her silence with her books, her silence alive with the freedom of her singing.

He wants to map her, still the song in her throat, tie the cloth of his will over her open eyes.

There is a struggle between the new and the old here, the struggle is between the old in him and the new in her.

My husband believes he is made of the new, the new-science, new-tech world, he is focused on the new, travels across continents to the new, gravitates toward the new. He drifts toward her because he smells the new on her, it draws him like Opium. He wants the new in her, he believes it is *His* because it is new, he sees himself after all as primordially drenched, soaked, enthroned in the new. He, he alone, is intended for all that is new, and nothing that is new can resist his steady advancing. The newness of her beckons, entices—it is a red flag on his own grounds, his own mansion, deep in the manor of his masculine illusions. He wants the newness of her to bend to his calling, his primary will, he wants the newness of her to acknowledge his steady staring, his smoking in her face beyond glass, back and forth, up and down, his beating down of her voice, her song. He wants the new in her so he can control, contain, tame, derail it. He wants the new in her to change in his hands like that, to be stripped, torn, shamed from its newness, to become the known, the familiar, the old.

Male, he knows he is intended alone for the new.

Female, she is marked, already staked for the old. *He wants to take the newness from her so she is made old in the taking.*

He will not have me become like her because I am already taken, and must stay as I am, part of the old, the known, the under control. *Taken taken taken.* No threat to other men, no face of the unknown to the world, no threat of other forays, other takings. *What to do to do* and *do as I say I say! You don't need to drive! You don't need to go out during the day!*

A single bird sings the same song, over and over.
     The same.
     What it comes down to is: he believes as male he is meant for the new; female, she is meant for the old.

Askew askew askew!

Same strophe of notes, same flicker of breath, same *repeat and pause, repeat and spill, repeat, repeat* from the bird's repeating throat.

*

The moment was full of a loud, insistent singing.

The bird extends, becomes a chorus. And I see my face in the mirror, I see the mirror's face, I see the mirror seeing: *bird sound call voice anew anew anew!*

And I see how I came to the same blue sky, miles away, years away, lands away from my home. The same blue sky that rules in the country of my childhood lurks above these trees—my husband wakes each day and brings it to me, he carried it with him through all the years of his growing-up, his coming to what he believed was *manhood*, his clinging to the old while he tilted, swung, unbalanced himself precariously toward the new.

I live in a new country, a country I did not think to come to, a country I believed would bring to me another life—a newness. And I live the oldness, the same life he would have me live in the country of our birth.

You wake to birds. You sleep. Birds in your waking, wake: a blanket of bird-call, a climb and flurry, rip at the center and spread the tear deep into sky—Virginia cardinal sky, redbud sky, new-arrival sky.

Where will I go? What will I do? Who will take care of me?

One call invokes another—one frenzy invites a third. The birds sing as if there is no tomorrow, or going beyond the singular moment. The singular moment alive with sound. The singular moment variously lifted, torn, broken through: sparrow, titmouse, cardinal, finch, nuthatch, tit, chickadee. Warble, flow, chirrup—steep and narrow, wide as a jar's open mouth, thin as strings of twisted metal.

*

Who will my daughter become? What world waits in the wings for her? What manner and shape of voice, what sound, what song?

Will she be pulled down deep into *the old, the old, the as-it's-always-been, the male dream*, or will she climb, fly, bird free to *the new the new the female new*?

I hear the train move on its tracks, I hear the wheels singing. I see how the platform starts to move and fly behind us, how the trees pursue its going. The room unwinds itself, unpins itself from its long trans-Atlantic fall of pleats, folds itself down in the distance. The smell of smoke borne away by wind, disappearing.

I am inside the moment of knowing.

*

Birds in a stream, river, water cascading millennially over *rock, rock, rock.* Tone and undertone, half and quarter, full, repeating, over, under—

the mirror looks at me full of eyes, full of speaking—

water water water blue blue blue and sky sky sky.